WHITE FIRE

FIRE

BRIAN

KEENE

deadite
press

deadite press

DEADITE PRESS
P.O. BOX 10065
PORTLAND, OR 97296
www.DEADITEPRESS.com

AN ERASERHEAD PRESS COMPANY
www.ERASERHEADPRESS.com

ISBN: 978-1-62105-277-7

Printed in the USA.

Thanks to Paul Goblirsch at Thunderstorm Books, Jeff Burk and Rose O'Keefe and everyone else at Deadite Press, Mike Oliveri, Mary SanGiovanni, and my sons.

For Steven L. Shrewsbury

1

"Check it out. Here comes another one."

Captain Tom Collins leaned close to the cargo van's passenger window and looked at the reflection in the side mirror. The black Saturn had fallen back several more car lengths, and the vehicles in the long line behind it were now too close together to count. There had been eighteen the last time he'd checked, and there were probably a few more now.

"A Saturn," he mumbled. "Do they even make parts for those things anymore?"

"We don't make anything anymore," Phil McLeod answered. "America is a service industry, now."

A red Grand Prix—the car that had initially caught their attention—eased out from behind the Saturn and into the other lane, then darted back again.

"We still make war," Collins replied.

"That we do." McLeod nodded, and glanced behind them. "And we make that, too. Our payload."

The red Grand Prix slid back into the lane and quickly gained on their van. Collins turned around in the seat and studied the people inside of the vehicle. A blonde girl sat in the passenger seat, her eyes wide—and a little scared. A pale, angry-looking kid with spiky hair and metal in his face scowled behind the steering wheel.

"So, what do you think?" Collins asked. "A passer or a fader?"

"The Grand Prix or the Saturn?"

"The Grand Prix."

McLeod's eyes darted from the road to the mirror and then back again. "Looks like a punk kid. Why do they do all that piercing shit? Whatever happened to a simple tattoo?"

"Everybody has tattoos now. Their parents are sporting ink. Hell, their grandparents in the old folks' homes have tattoos. They have to up the ante."

"I remember when a guy piercing his ear was a big deal. Now they've got dinner plates in their earlobes and shit sticking out of their lips."

"Come on, Phil," Collins insisted. "Passer or fader?"

McLeod frowned. "I'm going with passer. Illinois is flat. There are lots of straight-aways around here. He's used to passing."

"Another fiver? I'm up by fifteen bucks."

"What are you trying to say, Tom? I'm good for it!"

Collins grinned. "We'll see."

McLeod frowned. "We should go back to playing punch buggy."

The Grand Prix cruised right up to their back bumper. The kid peeked around the side, but oncoming traffic prevented him from passing and he eased back behind the van again. His lips mouthed curse words. Collins chuckled.

"What?" McLeod asked.

"He's back there cursing us out and…oh, wait a second. Here it comes. Here we go…"

Now came the moment of truth, as Collins referred to it. This was the moment where the driver spotted the government license plate and read the warning signs plastered all over the back of the van. Signs that said, *"This Vehicle Stops at All Railroad Crossings," "Keep Back 100 Feet,"* and, last but certainly not least, *"BIOHAZARD,"* complete with that jagged little symbol everyone recognized from album covers and horror movies.

The Grand Prix dropped its speed, falling back as the kid lost his nerve and let off the gas.

"I told you," Collins laughed. "He's a fader!"

"It's not fair," McLeod grumbled. "Look at the oncoming traffic. That fucking kid couldn't pass if he wanted to."

"You should've thought of that before you made the bet. But look at the bright side. We got another hundred miles or so ahead of us. That's plenty of time to earn your money back."

"I'm in deep enough, thank you very much."

"Shit, with that cushy private sector job? I thought you civilian contractor guys got paid the big bucks."

"Sure, if we ship out to Afghanistan or the Sudan or someplace like that. Not so much sub-contracting out to the Centers for Disease Control. What I should have done was taken the Alpinus gig instead."

"What's that?"

"Alpinus Biofutures. You've heard of them?"

Collins nodded. "Sure."

"They have an op going on right now in Mauritius."

"What kind of operation?"

McLeod side-eyed him. "You know better than that. I can't say. But my choices were that, or guarding some Saudi Arabian prince, or this."

Collins grinned. "And you took this gig because you love me."

"I took this gig because it kept me close to home. And yeah, you're okay. We've worked well together before. Just don't take all my money. I don't have that fat-ass Army salary to draw on like some people I could mention."

Collins shook his head. "It's not what it used to be, my friend."

"No?"

"Definitely no. Especially with my ex-wife and two teenage kids sucking half off the top. It pisses me off. The only time I hear from them is when they need money—money on top of what I pay every month."

McLeod sighed, and gripped the steering wheel a little

harder. "Glad my engagement fell apart last month."

"Oh man, I'm sorry to hear that. What happened?"

"Let's just say I caught my fiancé sucking something, too. But it wasn't money, and it sure as hell wasn't mine."

Collins gasped in surprise. "Toby? No way!"

McLeod nodded, gripping the wheel a little tighter.

"Ahh. That's messed up, Phil. Toby seemed like a nice guy. I liked him."

McLeod grunted. "Yeah, that's the problem. A lot of other guys liked him, too."

"Shit…"

"It's my own fault," McLeod said. "There's been trouble between us for a while. Lots of stress. My folks didn't like him. His folks didn't like me. Sometimes I think we'd have been better off if everyone had stayed in the closet. Might have been easier if they'd just believed we were roommates. Plus, my mother was adamant about wanting grandbabies… the whole thing was fucked. But, I figured I'd stick with jobs that kept me here in the States. Thought if I spent more time with him that things might…improve."

Collins nodded. "Yeah…I used to think that way, too, when my marriage with Cheryl was falling apart. At least you dodged that bullet."

They grew quiet. The radio played softly in the background. Both men shared a fondness for country music, and in the last hour, they'd discovered a station playing the classics. Kenny Rogers begged Ruby not to take her love to town, and Merle Travis's "Divorce Me C.O.D." segued into Loretta Lynn's "Somebody Somewhere (Don't Know What He's Missing Tonight)." After a while, Collins began to hum along. By the time Waylon Jennings began his ode to Luckenbach, Texas, both men were singing. The tires hummed on the pavement, and road signs flashed by. The line of cars stretched out behind them.

A fat raindrop struck the windshield, followed by another

and another. They sounded like rocks falling from the sky. Collins leaned forward and peered upward. A series of dark, ominous thunderheads rolled in from the west, pushing through the sky like a steamroller. More drops pelted the windshield.

McLeod turned down the radio, and turned on the headlights and wipers. "I thought your people said this storm would miss us?"

"They did."

"Mm. Maybe it was the same team who found those weapons of mass destruction in Iraq, eh? Good old military intelligence."

Collins shot him a dirty look, but McLeod had turned his attention back to the road, obviously trying hard to focus on driving as the wind picked up and buffeted the van. The old Dodge Lunchbox wasn't designed to be sleek, and McLeod let off the gas and gripped the wheel with both hands. His knuckles popped. Leaves and debris blew across the highway, and a crumpled cigarette pack ricocheted off the top of the windshield.

Then the clouds exploded, and the downpour began—a heavy, driving rain that smeared the road and oncoming headlights into muted blobs of color. The steady pounding on the roof drowned out the radio, and McLeod decreased their speed even further. Collins checked the rearview mirror, but couldn't make out anything past the back of the van. The wind rocked them back and forth.

"Shit," McLeod groaned.

"Bad?" Collins asked.

McLeod gestured out the windshield as the wind forced them toward the side of the road. He swerved back out again. A car horn blared behind them.

"This is nuts," McLeod said. "I thought it only rained like this in the mountains."

"Don't worry, it can't last long."

"Why not?"

"These storms never do. Just a couple of minutes and then—"

A bright flash illuminated the windshield, turning it into a solid wall of light for a fraction of a second. The thunderclap blasted their ears before the lightning's afterimage had faded from their retinas.

"Jesus!" McLeod shouted. "What the fuck?"

The van shivered and swerved again beneath them.

"Relax, Phil. Just relax. Deep breaths, man."

"Fucking 'Relax' he says. You know goddamn well what we're hauling!"

"Which is exactly why I don't want you to run us off the road and let this shit loose on the highway."

"I'm not trying to run us off the highway! The storm is. Maybe if we pulled over for a bit?"

"Not with our cargo. Now calm down and get a hold of yourself."

The field to their right erupted in white light. The resulting thunder shook the van, rocking it on its frame.

"Sorry," McLeod apologized. "But I'd be a lot less nervous if I could just frigging *see...*"

Eventually, the rain slowed to a steady patter. The windshield cleared, and a pair of cars further up the road who pulled off the shoulder during the worst of the storm, now eased back onto the road and resumed driving.

Collins wondered if he'd made the right call. Maybe it would have been a good idea for he and McLeod to stop, as well. Then he looked over at the deep trenches running along the side of the road and changed his mind. If McLeod lost his way and dumped them into the six-foot rivulet, there would be no driving out of it. Several inches of rain—runoff from the road and the bean field next to it—already coursed along the bottom of the nearest trench.

"I guess you were right, Tom," McLeod admitted.

"How's that?"

"You said it would only last a few minutes. It looks like someone upstairs was listening."

"I didn't know you were religious, Phil."

McLeod shrugged. "I am when it suits me—when I need something. Isn't it that way with most people?"

"I guess. I just figured…"

"What?"

"Well, you know, with you being gay and all. I figured religion wouldn't exactly be your thing."

"Oh, come on, Tom. That's like saying there's no gay Conservatives. We're people, just like anybody else. Some of us are religious. I mean, don't get me wrong. I don't go to church, and I don't thump the bible. I'm not crazy about their official views on marriage and stuff, but I like to believe there's something out there. Something more than this. Don't you?"

"I don't know," Collins admitted. "I guess maybe I'm agnostic."

"So, you believe in something, then. You're not an atheist, right?"

"I don't know what the hell I am anymore. At one time? Sure. I believed. But that was a long time ago. My mother was a believer. She used to take me to church every Sunday. And then she died."

"You were still a kid then, right?"

Collins nodded. "I was. Hell, her death is why I do what I do now, as an adult. If she hadn't contracted AIDS from that transfusion…who knows what I'd be doing now. But she did, and here I am. I stopped believing when she passed, and I haven't seen much since then that makes me rethink things."

"Maybe you just need to look harder."

"Yeah, maybe." Shrugging, Collins looked out the window and shivered.

On the radio, Johnny Cash sang about ghost riders in the sky.

"Here we go." McLeod began to speed up again. "This is much better."

"It doesn't look much better." Collins stared at the sky, which had taken on a strange, green color. It looked... unhealthy. The clouds overhead chased one another in a tight circle.

Johnny Cash gave way to a series of loud, urgent tones, which sounded like a dying bird. Shuffling papers followed, and the disc jockey cleared his throat. He sounded nervous. "This is the Emergency Broadcast System. I repeat, this is the County Emergency Broadcast System. This is not a test. The National Weather Service has announced a tornado warning..."

"So much for that," McLeod said. "Christ!"

Collins watched the wounded sky. "Just keep cool and drive."

They listened as the announcer rattled off a long list of counties and towns, and shelters.

McLeod jumped in his seat. "Did he just say Newton? We drove through there a little while ago."

Collins ignored him and turned up the radio.

The announcer continued listing names, then talked about high winds, hail, and severe thunderstorms. He paused for a moment, and then said, "This just in—we have confirmation of a tornado touchdown east of Godfrey. I repeat, the National Weather Service confirms a tornado is on the ground east of Godfrey. Listeners in the area should seek shelter immediately."

Both men turned and stared at each other in concern.

"Shit!" McLeod whistled. "The cargo. What do we do, Tom?"

"Hang on." Paper rustled as Collins hastily unfolded a map. He traced the road with his finger. "Godfrey's only a few miles ahead of us. Make for that."

An ear-splitting wail suddenly filled the air.

"What the hell is that?" McLeod shouted.

Collins spotted a siren on top of a utility pole up ahead. The sound raised in pitch as the cone rotated in their direction.

"Emergency siren," he told McLeod.

"It's fucking loud!"

Collins craned his neck to see out the window better. Though he wouldn't know a funnel cloud from a thunderhead, he knew damn well he'd recognize a twister if he saw one. He glanced behind them. Traffic had all but disappeared, including the long line of cars that had been following them up until the storm hit. They were alone on the road.

"Wonderful. Just fucking wonderful." Sweat trickled down the side of McLeod's face. He slapped the thermostat switch as far over to the blue as it would go, and then wrenched the fan speed to high.

"You okay?" Collins asked, genuinely concerned.

McLeod nodded. "Chest pains."

"Oh no…"

"No, it's not a heart attack. Just stress and the heat."

"Let's just keep our heads together." Collins own heart beat faster. He folded up the map and stuffed it into the glove compartment.

The radio went dead, cutting off the disc jockey in mid-sentence. Collins scanned the dial, but could find no other stations that were broadcasting.

They slowly approached a crossroads, and Collins spotted a Jeep parked about a hundred yards to the right of the intersection. It was alone, with no other vehicles in sight. The Jeep's muted green paint scheme nearly blended in with the cornfield on the far side of the road, but the driver could not be missed. He wore a long, pale overcoat and leaned against the winch mounted to the front bumper. He crossed his arms over his broad chest and open jacket, as if defying the rain, and his head turned to follow the van as it approached the intersection. His long, stark white hair, the color of corn silk, fell way past his shoulders, and was dripping wet. His eyes and cheekbones looked stark and sunken, and his complexion was as pale as his coat.

"I think we can make it to the next town," McLeod said. His eyes were glued to the road ahead, and Collins could tell that he didn't notice the strange man. "We'll be safer there."

The man in the pale overcoat pushed off from the Wrangler and took three steps closer to the road. Smiling, he stood at attention, and then snapped off a sharp military salute.

"Hmm." Collins squinted at the figure. "That's weird."

"What's weird? Are you listening to me, Tom?"

"Don't worry about it," Collins said. "We're fine right where we are. The odds are a million to one against that we actually get hit by a tornado, and besides, if we're in the middle of town and a tornado touches down there, we—"

Lightning flared overhead again, bathing the nearby field with stark illumination. In the flash, the man in the overcoat's face dissolved into a garish, leering skull. A large pair of pale, feathery wings unfurled from his back and stretched far over his head. Collins blinked. The lightning flash faded. The stranger was just a man again, still standing at attention.

"What the hell..."

"What is it?" McLeod's voice crackled with panic, and he damn near pressed his forehead to the windshield as he looked up at the sky. "What's wrong with you, Tom? Is it a tornado?"

They sped through the intersection and the man turned his back on them and walked back to the Jeep. His shoulders shook, as if he were laughing.

"Tom! Are you having a stroke? What the fuck is the matter with you?"

"I...Sorry. The lightning blinded me for a second. I was

saying we'd be better off staying out of town. If it gets hit, there's going to be a lot of debris. Not to mention our cargo."

"You're not alleviating my stress." McLeod took one hand off the steering wheel long enough to wipe his sweaty palm on the thigh of his jeans. Then he did the same with the other hand.

Collins took a deep breath and exhaled. "Back there, did you see—"

Another wail sounded behind them.

McLeod frowned. "Is that the sirens again?"

Collins twisted toward the window and looked behind them. "I'm not sure. It sounds almost like a jet engine, doesn't it?"

"Sort of." McLeod scowled. "But on the highway?"

Collins glanced out the passenger window. They passed a farmhouse with a large yard. A rickety barn with peeling green paint leaned hard to the left, barely sheltering a green John Deere tractor from the rain. More green suddenly swirled through the air, and it took Collins a second to recognize the streaks as uprooted cornstalks. Shingles flew off the barn roof, then an entire wooden panel, and then the back of the barn exploded as a massive gray column plowed its way through the yard.

"Oh shit," Collins shouted. "Phil…"

"I see it!"

"Floor it! Get us the hell out of here."

The van's engine grumbled, but they rocketed forward. Rain splattered the windshield, and puddles disintegrated into high fans of mist beneath their tires. Both men kept their eyes on the rear-view mirrors, and as a result they didn't see the little blue coupe flying toward the next intersection.

"Shit!" McLeod slammed on the brakes.

The tires screeched and skidded, then hydroplaned across the standing water. The rear end slalomed across the yellow dividing line and McLeod wrenched the wheel back and forth. Collins nearly punctured the faux leather seats with his fingernails.

The coupe zipped into the intersection, the driver hunched over the wheel and oblivious to their presence until their headlights shone across the side of his face. A heavy splash washed over the van's windshield and the car was gone. The van slid sideways and skidded. Collins gritted his teeth and stood on an imaginary brake as they passed the intersection and missed the blue coupe's rear end by inches. Collins tensed, his muscles taught. The van lurched to the side and Collins' shoulder hit the window.

"Please don't roll oh shit please don't roll baby come on," McLeod pleaded. He pulled the wheel around to the right again and mashed the gas. The van righted itself with a thud and bounced. McLeod quickly shifted both feet to the brake pedal. The van, still wiggling on its suspension, shuddered to a stop.

Both men sat in silence for a few seconds. The only sound was their heavy breathing. The radio came back on with a commercial for a car dealership. It seemed surreal.

"You okay, Tom?"

"Yeah," Collins said. "How about you?"

"Yeah. I'm good. Is it over? Did it pass us?"

Collins saw only darkness reflected in the mirror, and then they both heard the ominous freight train-like roar bearing down on them.

"Go, Phil! Fucking go!"

McLeod floored it. The wheels spun on the wet pavement, caught, and then hovered as the twister lifted the ass end of the van into the air. Collins once again clung to the seat while McLeod frantically shifted and mashed the pedals. The van whipped sideways and drifted across the oncoming lane, dragging the front wheels the whole way. The tornado slammed the rear end down. The driver's side rear tire dipped into the drainage ditch and the whole rear corner dangled over the side. They hung there for a second, teetering on the brink with the winds shoving against the broad side of the van.

Collins felt the crown on his molar shatter as he pressed himself into his seat, trying to make weight. He dared not even breathe lest the slightest motion topple them. The tornado howled in his ear, hammering his window. Rocks and gravel pelted the cabin like bullets. The landscape beyond the windshield—at least, what little he could see of it—rocked like the horizon on his brother's twenty-foot fishing boat in moderate swells.

The tornado tore at the top of the van. The roof bowed out, crackling and popping with the pressure. The metal groaned.

You can't lift us, Collins thought. *If you could, you would have, and we'd be halfway into that field by now. We're gonna make it.*

But the tornado didn't need lift. It skirted across the road in front of them and sandblasted the centerlines right off the asphalt in a whirling cloud of dirt and grit, flaying the paint off the side. The funnel cloud delivered one final shove. The van tilted as its weight shifted, and then toppled over the edge.

Collins' stomach rolled. His seatbelt cinched tight and squeezed the air out of him, and his camouflage standard BDU cap flew away. The driver's side door struck the inside slope. The side mirror shattered and collapsed, punching through the window and slicing McLeod's upper arm and shoulder. His scream was lost beneath the shriek of tortured metal and the tornado's howl.

The van's momentum carried it over onto its roof. The rear end struck first, then the front slammed down. Their lap belts bit into their hips and Collins' toe struck something hard on the underside of the console. His yelp came out as little more than a gasp.

Somewhere in the back of the van, there was a crunching sound.

Water gushed around the frame where the driver's side window had been only minutes before. McLeod clutched his arm and hissed with pain. Blood dripped through his fingers and drew wispy red clouds in the water.

Collins felt his big toe swelling to fill his boot, and he spat out his crown, and tasted blood. A cursory check told him he was fine, otherwise. The seatbelt latch clung stubbornly, until he pushed against the roof with one hand to take some of his weight off the belt. The latch finally gave, and he tumbled onto his shoulder, wincing with pain.

"Phil," he shouted over the wind, "are you okay?"

McLeod's face was pale and beaded with blood and sweat. "I…"

Collins slid on his shoulder blades across the ceiling beneath McLeod. His jacket soaked up the cold water and chilled his back. He shivered.

McLeod stared down at his wound. "I don't know…"

"Let me see." Collins gently took hold of McLeod's injured arm. "Are you hurt anywhere else?"

"No, I don't think so."

"All right. This is going to hurt a little. Just keep still, okay?"

McLeod nodded. A second later, he howled as Collins kneaded his arm, but did not pull it away.

"It's not broken," Collins reported. "You've got some deep lacerations, and we'll have to pick out the glass."

"You're just full of good news, Tom."

"Well, you're not gonna bleed out. At least not right away. Does that help?"

Suddenly, another crash shook the van, hard enough to bounce Collins off the ceiling. He knocked the back of his head against the top.

"Oh, son of a bitch!"

McLeod jumped. "What the hell was that?"

"I'm not sure." Groaning, Collins pushed away from McLeod and sat up. "I hope it wasn't lightning."

"The gas tank," McLeod said. "We might be on fire!"

Collins leaned toward the window. "I don't think so. I can't see anything. Next time I'll have to requisition a van with a damn window into the cargo area."

"Would you not worry about that now?" McLeod's voice was high and shrill as he yanked on his seatbelt. "Get me the hell out of here. I don't want to burn!"

"Stop it, Phil." Collins grabbed the front of his shirt and stared into his eyes. "Just relax. We're not on fire. You're okay."

"I need to get out of here, man! Please?"

"Okay, hold on." Collins pressed his chest to McLeod's and pushed him back and up against the seat. He thumbed the seatbelt release and caught McLeod, then eased him down. McLeod grunted as he rolled over his arm, until the two men sat together on the ceiling.

The freight train noise faded, and the wind sounded like an open car window on the highway. The pitch dropped, and within seconds everything went silent. A few loose pieces of gravel plopped into the water outside, and a handful of leaves fluttered to the ground.

"It's over." McLeod sighed heavily and leaned against his seat. "Thank God."

Collins rolled his head from side to side, cracking his joints. "I'm going to check the damage."

"Okay. Be careful."

The window and door locks wouldn't respond to their respective buttons, so Collins popped the glove compartment and removed his sidearm, a Kimber 1911. He tossed the holster aside and checked the .45's chamber, made sure the safety was on, and then used the barrel to knock out the passenger window. He cleared the top—now bottom—rim of glass, then shimmied through the opening and up the outer slope of the ditch. Glass crunched beneath his knees. He spotted his wayward BDU cap and retrieved it. The cloth was soaking wet. He wrung it out and donned it again. Then he looked around.

It only took one glance to assess the damage.

"Oh shit. Oh no…"

"Is it…?" McLeod asked. He sounded afraid. "Don't tell me it's…?"

Collins turned back to face him. Lightning flashed again, illuminating his terrified expression.

"We've got a breach," he whispered. "It's loose."

2

The tornado rolled into Godfrey, Illinois like a rampaging steamroller driven by a malicious child, and left a vicious path of destruction in its wake.

It started on the south edge of town, where it mowed through Oliver Michael's herd of dairy cows, hurling them spinning into the sky and then pelting them down in a hail of wet, red meat. It tore through Oliver's barn, then ripped up the grove of trees and a fence line, before turning toward the town proper.

The tornado churned down Spike Street, where it turned three old houses into matchsticks and sheared the second stories off two more homes. A stop sign became a torpedo, spearing through a smiling politician's billboard, leaving a large, gaping hole in the politician's face. Later, some residents would agree that it was an improvement.

Turning onto Pine Street, the funnel cloud ripped off entire rooftops and scattered them like rain. It dropped massive trees on top of cars, and tossed the Jacobs family's doghouse through their neighbor's big bay window. The dog was thrown even further. The old bell at St. Mary's church rang one last time as it landed on the concrete walk out front, cracking the cement into fragments and breaking a water main.

The maelstrom lingered at the intersection of Pine Street and Lake Avenue, churning over an alley occupied by Godfrey's sole homeless citizen, an unfortunate soul named Norwood. At age forty-one, Norwood had bounced around between group homes and family members, most recently living in his grandparent's basement. Since their deaths, he'd been sleeping in the woods on the outskirts of town when the weather was nice, and between two garbage dumpsters in the alley when the weather turned bad. He'd been asleep when the weather turned very bad indeed, and didn't wake up until the howling winds first caressed his face, tossing his dirty black locks of hair into his rheumy eyes. Then, flailing helplessly, Norwood was yanked into the sky, along with his few meager possessions, the garbage dumpsters, and the roof of a nearby storage facility. He gaped as the air rushed from his lungs, and thus, was unable to scream as a sheet of corrugated metal cut him in half at the waist. Norwood turned into a fine, red mist.

The tornado zigzagged for two blocks, then made a sharp right turn and wound its way up Main Street, carving a swath through the asphalt and throwing power lines around like limp spaghetti noodles. Telephone poles snapped and splintered. The funnel blew out windows and doors, shredded more roofs, and sucked three tables, four chairs, and a flyer for the American Legion's pancake breakfast out of O'Reilly's Tap, a local tavern. The venerable old oak tree in the town square, that dated back to before the Civil War, toppled over, taking out the facade of Mariotte's Fine Foods and creating front-page photos and video bumpers for newspapers and television broadcasts across the country. The tornado imploded the post office, but left the shiny blue mailbox to stand proud out in front of the ruins. The used bookstore vanished, replaced by a crater and some shards of broken plumbing. The gourmet coffee shop was reduced to rubble. A four-story red brick boarding house remained standing, but lost every one of its windows.

Next, the funnel snaked across Poplar Street and worked its way diagonally to Maple. Pete Zedlacher's mulch pile became fodder for the wind. The gale tore the sides off the Morgan's brand-new swimming pool and the subsequent deluge flooded their basement. Then the tornado picked up their neighbor's rickety metal shed and distributed the top and sides like playing cards. The gardening tools inside of the shed flew apart like shrapnel from a grenade and buried themselves in homes, vehicles, and trees. A shovel shot through a mobile camper, and a sickle stuck so deeply and firmly in a denuded old maple tree that future owners would dub it Excalibur.

The tornado took another abrupt turn—this time heading north along Commerce Street. It smashed the carports of both the Ford dealership and the gas station, and then hopped the rickety fence to the lumberyard behind the hardware store. The fence remained standing. The hardware store did not. The order of 2x4s for the Meadows family's new home construction had just been loaded, and the teenagers working the lot were more interested in grabbing a few tokes of marijuana behind the barn than tying the load down, so they used old bailing twine and tied haphazard knots. The tornado flung some of the studs as far as two miles away, including one that landed on top of Steve Atlas's grain silo, right next to the corpse of a deer which had been blown up top, as well. The deer was not the only animal to fall victim to the funnel cloud. In addition to it, Oliver Michael's herd of cows and the Jacobs family's dog—a horse, two more cows, five goats, fourteen stray cats, more than five-dozen squirrels, countless birds, and several skunks, rabbits, groundhogs, and foxes were tossed like rag dolls before crashing back to the ground in broken, battered, bloody heaps.

A few more twists and turns brought the funnel in contact with a deli, a Chinese restaurant, a laundromat, and the garage of Kevin Delaroz. The contents of the first three were deposited in the latter, demolishing it, along with all of the equipment Delaroz used to record his Alt-Right podcast. A replica Nazi swastika banner with a leering frog emblazoned upon it, which had hung from the garage wall, was sent hurtling into the air and landed on a distant rooftop. Later, emerging from his basement, Delaroz fell to his knees in a puddle and wept over the loss.

The storm then leveled all of the homes on one side of Maple Street, decimating an entire block. It also managed to pick up the sidewalk and fling slabs of concrete into the air. Then it dug deeper, ripping up utility cables and pipes and sent them skyward, as well.

Finally, the tornado neared the other side of Godfrey, and flattened the four-acre trailer park. Not a single mobile home escaped the fray. Fragments of fabricated housing were strewn around like Legos. The park manager's office had a basement, and the residents cowered together there, listening as everything they owned was pulverized and scattered.

After that, the funnel made its way toward the Shady Acres Nursing Home. Watching from his window after hiding out when the rest of the residents were herded into the storm cellar, Mr. Chester Nesmith, now in his tenth year of residence, wished he had the strength to walk outside and let the twister take him away. Later, he would dream about this and smile in his sleep.

The tornado churned in place in front of the nursing home, as if deciding where to go next. Slowly, its speed decreased. It moved forward, prying a few pieces of vinyl siding off the building and uprooting a well-maintained line of shrubbery. Its speed continued to steadily decline. Almost as an afterthought, the funnel cloud dismantled the jungle gym in the community playground across the street, tossed some mulch into the air, tiptoed across the well-manicured lawn, then petered out and receded into the sky. The nursing home's management didn't even bother to submit the cost of the three pieces of damaged siding or the shrubbery to the insurance company. Later, old Mrs. Webster wondered why the kids didn't play across the street anymore. Watching them climb on the jungle gym had always made her think of the grandchildren she'd never had.

When it was all over, Father Deane, the priest at St. Mary's, praised God that so few townspeople were killed, especially given the massive devastation left behind in the storm's wake. Reverend Anderson, the pastor of the Baptist church, said the tornado was a sign of the Lord's wrath, that it was divine retribution for the adult DVD and bookstore just across the highway, and the fact that the Godfrey Junior High school had copies of the *Harry Potter* books in their library. Both the school library and the adult bookstore survived the storm unscathed. The Baptist church did not. Bob Trimble, the owner of the adult bookstore, used a segment of one of the Meadows family's wall studs—which he found lying in his parking lot—to scare the fire and brimstone out of a handful of Baptist looters.

Within an hour, the media descended on the town like a swarm of locusts, and set up camp in the very heart of the destruction. Reporters from Fox News, CNN, MSNBC, The Weather Channel, and the local stations jostled each other for the best footage and interviews. The first news crew on the scene found toothless Murray "Red" Swanson sifting through the rubble, and interviewed him. Murray referred to the tornado as "The Big 'Un." The name stuck, though the newswires re-dubbed it "The Big One." Headlines were written both ways. A popular actor promised on social media to organize a televised benefit event (in New York or Los Angeles, rather than at ground zero), and the President of the United States offered his prayers and sympathies to the survivors. The residents of Godfrey didn't need either. They constantly lived with the knowledge that they were smack dab in the middle of tornado alley, and they knew how to handle themselves when severe weather struck. In all, only six people were killed, and a dozen injured. Several hundred found themselves homeless, and a many more would deal with leaky roofs and broken windows until the insurance checks cleared.

But all in all, the mayor said into a television camera, it could have been worse.

And then it was.

The tornado was just the beginning for Godfrey, Illinois—the calm before the storm.

3

Collins and McLeod stood at the top of the ditch and stared down at the van. Collins grimaced, and spat blood again. The pain in his big toe had subsided, but his tooth hurt. He kept prodding it with his tongue, almost uncontrollably, and then hissing with pain. McLeod trembled, clutching his bleeding arm. A steady rain pattered across their heads. Collins wrung out his camouflage cap, stared at it, and then put it back on anyway.

"You really think it got out?" McLeod toyed with the gauze around his wounded arm. His face and lips were alabaster.

Collins hoped his companion was just terrified, and not going into shock. They had enough problems. McLeod had remained remarkably calm while Collins had picked broken glass and debris from the wounded man's arm, barely wincing, even though Collins had used his fingers and they had no painkillers.

"The cargo," McLeod said, when Collins didn't answer. "Do you really think it got out?"

"Oh, I'm pretty sure it got out, Phil."

In fact, he had no doubt the virus they were transporting to a CDC-designated facility near Morris, Illinois, had been released. A massive ceiling beam impaled the van, effectively pinning it to the side of the ditch. That explained the last crash they'd heard. The beam had also passed through the refrigerated container, and there was sparkling, broken glass everywhere. He stared at the gaping hole in the side of the container, and shivered.

"Well," McLeod moaned, "you sound pretty goddamned calm about it."

"What's the point of panicking?" Collins shook his head. "Screaming won't help our situation now."

"How did it break through, Tom?"

"You can see the damage same as I can." Collins raised an eyebrow. "I hear tornadoes can bury blades of grass in trees. This is nothing."

"Yeah, but don't you guys take precautions against this shit?"

"The cabin's reinforced against accidents, sure. But it's only a van, Phil, not an Abrams tank! We got hit by a fucking tornado."

"Well, maybe we should have had a tank!"

"Stealth was the order of the day. They didn't want to transport this with a military convoy. That's why they subcontracted with your outfit. The point was to blend in with everyone else on the road and not attract attention."

"Yeah, I guess." McLeod worked his jaw as he considered that. "Can I ask you something?"

"Sure."

"Do you think we're infected?"

Collins sighed. "It's hard to say."

"Try anyway."

"I don't know. I really don't."

"Try harder."

Collins hesitated. "We could be."

McLeod turned even paler. "Fuck me…"

Collins nodded in agreement.

"So," McLeod asked, "what do we do?"

Collins took his cell phone out of his pocket. He had no signal bars, but the screen didn't say 'No Service.' Mouthing a silent plea, he thumbed the speed dial for one of the base numbers, but only got a fast-busy signal. Disgusted, he shoved the phone back in his pocket.

McLeod looked hopeful. "Anything?"

"No. The storm must have messed up all the lines or knocked out a cell tower or something. We're going to have to hoof it into town and notify emergency services."

"What about the emergency radio in the van?"

"It's fucked."

"We're fucked," McLeod whispered.

Collins didn't disagree with him. He crawled back into the wreckage and fetched his holster. He secured it and the pistol to his belt, then pulled the thick sheaf of his orders off the clipboard, rolled them up, and tucked them into his thigh pocket. He wished he had a better way to secure the van, but felt confident the biohazard warnings would keep all but the most curious of passerby away.

"You still got your sidearm?" Collins asked.

McLeod nodded. "Yeah, but my aim is gonna be for shit."

"Hopefully, we won't need it."

They started walking. Collins stuck to McLeod's left side so that he could keep a better eye on him. Blood already soaked the gauze from the first aid kit, but not so much that it dripped or flowed through. They would still need to get McLeod to a doctor, but the wound wasn't life threatening. As they walked, the color even returned to his face and lips, suggesting that maybe his problem was more fear than shock.

Collins couldn't blame him for being scared. He was terrified, too.

It's out, he thought. *Holy shit, the scenario we train for, the one that's never supposed to happen, has happened. The virus is loose. VM2 is out. I'm trying to put up this brave face for Phil, but the shit is loose...*

He sucked air, and the nerves in his tooth sent a lance of pain through his head. Collins grunted, wincing again. He spat one more time, but his saliva was only pink now, rather than red.

"You okay?" McLeod asked.

"The crash knocked one of my crowns off my teeth. I'll be fine, though. We've got more important things to worry about."

"Yeah," McLeod agreed. "I guess we do."

They stepped over a thick, fallen tree limb. One end was a splintered ruin. So was the rest of the countryside. The tornado had cut a swath of destruction around them. The fields looked as though Stevie Wonder had taken a harvester combine for a drunken joyride. Leaves and cornstalks lay strewn across the road. The power lines running along the northbound lane had all been ripped down, and the crossbeams were torn off the tops of some of the poles. Collins had never seen anything like it. It surprised him that they'd survived it, especially after watching that barn blow apart.

"Man…"

"What's up?" McLeod asked.

"Oh," Collins sighed. "I was just thinking how lucky we are to be walking away at all. That makes twice for me now."

"Twice?"

"Yeah. Between this tornado and a chopper accident in Nigeria that I walked away from two years ago, I imagine that my guardian angel must be working overtime to earn his paycheck."

"I thought you didn't believe in that stuff?"

Before Collins could respond, the throaty rumble of an engine approached them from behind. They turned as a primer-colored, rickety pick-up truck weaved around the tree limb and pulled along beside them. An old man with coarse, salt and pepper stubble and wearing a faded hunting hat leaned out the cab window and spat a stream of tobacco juice.

"Hey there." His expression was concerned. "You fellas okay? Need a lift?"

"Hi." Collins smiled. "You wouldn't happen to have a cell phone we could use, would you? Mine's on the fritz."

"Nope." The old man shook his head. "My daughter tried to buy me one last Christmas, but I wouldn't have nothing to do with it. Damn things give you brain cancer. But I'd be glad to give you a ride into Godfrey."

Collins glanced into the truck's bed. It was full of split firewood, and there was no room for them there. They'd have to sit up front. He debated the wisdom of climbing into the truck and possibly infecting the old man with the virus, but he needed to contact his superiors, and McLeod needed medical attention for his arm. And if they were now carrying the virus, they would be putting others at risk the moment they set foot in town anyway. It was probably too late, in any case. His main priority at this point was contacting his superiors and letting them know everything had gone balls up.

Stepping forward, Collins dug his nails into the palm of his hand to keep from screaming. It was like he'd been telling McLeod. Remaining calm was the only option they had right now, no matter how badly he wanted to collapse into a ball right there alongside the road and weep.

The urge to do so was very strong.

"T-tom...?"

McLeod's voice was weak and quavering. Collins turned back to him.

"If we've been exposed," McLeod whispered, "then won't we infect him, too?"

Sighing, Collins nodded. "Yes. Yes, we would. But we've got no choice, Phil. We are now racing against the clock. We need to focus on quarantine and containment. We take this opportunity, hold him when we arrive, and then if he is impacted by exposure to us..."

"The cavalry can help him when they get here?"

Collins smiled. "Sure."

Opening the door, he thanked the old man, helped McLeod into the truck, and then slid in beside him. A plastic Jesus on the dashboard held out his welcoming arms, and the cab smelled like a combination of black licorice and Copenhagen tobacco. It was cold inside the cab. The air conditioning was on full blast. The radio was tuned to a conservative talk show. Collins didn't recognize the host, but assumed it was syndicated, since there was no mention of the tornado.

"You fellas were whispering amongst yourselves," the old man observed. "Don't worry. I ain't one of those serial killers, if that's what's got you wondering."

Collins grinned. "How do you know we're not?"

The old man nodded at Collins's uniform. "Dressed like that?"

The truck sputtered and then lurched forward. Collins felt cold air blowing on him, and realized that the old man had the air conditioning cranked. McLeod shivered next to him. He thought about asking the good Samaritan to turn it down, but before he could the old man spoke again.

"So, what branch are you boys with?"

"Army," Collins replied.

"You, too?" The old man nodded at McLeod's jeans and t-shirt.

"No," McLeod said. "I'm a...civilian contractor."

"Like them people from Haliburton?"

"Something like that. Not Haliburton, though. Different outfit."

The old man frowned. His bottom lip stuck out, concealing a tobacco plug. "You're not one of those Blackwater assholes, are you?"

"No, nothing like that! Fuck those guys."

"Damn straight," the old man agreed. "I quit voting Republican after the mess those assholes made in Iraq."

Despite his injuries and fears, McLeod chuckled. "I

was enlisted at one time. Now I specialize in transportation. Currently, I'm freelancing for the CDC."

"Well, thank you both for your service." The old man clacked his false teeth together. "I was in the Navy myself. Signalman. Served up and down the Mekong, back in sixty-eight and sixty-nine."

"You were a river rat?" Collins asked.

"Goddamn right I was. Never saw any other water other than brown."

"Respect."

The old man grinned. "Name's Richard Nagle. Always happy to help out a fellow service man."

"I'm Captain Tom Collins. This is Phil."

"We appreciate it, Mr. Nagle," McLeod said, shivering.

"So...what's an Army captain and a CDC mercenary doing in rural Illinois, if you don't mind my asking?"

"We're both on loan to the CDC right now," McLeod answered, "but that's really all we can say."

"Is there a hospital in Godfrey?" Collins asked, trying to change the subject.

"No, sir. But I can take you to the fire department."

"That would be great. I'm going to need to talk to the emergency services people as soon as possible."

"That got anything to do with the biohazard signs all over your van back yonder?"

Collins pursed his lips and said nothing.

"Thought as much," Nagle mused. "Figured it had to be your vehicle the moment I saw you. How bad? What are we looking at?"

Out of the corner of his eye, Collins saw McLeod's head turn toward him.

"We can get a handle on it if we move fast," Collins said. "But the clock is ticking."

"Roger that." Nagle pressed the pedal to the floor and the engine roared a little louder. "She'll do fifty-five, maybe even sixty. Not that I drive that fast. But this is an exception. Don't guess you can tell me what you boys were carrying?"

Collins shook his head apologetically. "I'm sorry. That's classified."

Mr. Nagle nodded. "I figured as much. Probably better if you don't tell me, anyway."

"You're right," McLeod said. "You don't want to know."

Mr. Nagle focused on the road and urged the truck forward. Moments later, sirens sounded behind them, and the old man drifted to the shoulder. A fire engine streaked by, followed closely by an ambulance. The name on the side of the ambulance was Warren-something, and Collins suspected neighboring communities were sending help. He made a mental note to discuss the handling of emergency personnel coming and going.

Mr. Nagle started moving again, and the emergency vehicles quickly receded into the distance. Collins wished they had stayed put a moment longer and caught a ride with them. The truck creaked and groaned.

"Uh oh," the old man said, and this time hugged the shoulder but did not stop. "Here comes another one."

A familiar green Jeep shot past them, and Collins caught a brief glance of the gaunt driver and his fluttering pale overcoat. The strange man saluted them again, and then rocketed out of sight. Before he disappeared, Collins noticed that he was grinning.

McLeod noticed the expression on Collins's face. "Who was that?"

"He was a damn fool," Nagle muttered. "He's gonna kill somebody, driving around like that."

McLeod tapped Collins on the shoulder. "Did you know him?"

Collins shook his head. "I...back before we crashed, I..."

"Yep." The old man wheeled back out onto the road.

"That idiot will be the death of us all, if we ain't careful."

Collins remembered how the Jeep-man's face had looked like a skull, right before the tornado hit, and wondered if Mr. Nagle was right.

4

With the containment and cooling system destroyed by the ceiling beam, and its vials shattered, the virus had quickly warmed and took flight. Colorless and odorless, it diffused in the humid, post-storm stillness, and both men had gotten a good, strong whiff of it.

Richard Nagle always drove with the air-conditioning as cold as it would go, even in the dead of winter. If he'd had his way before his wife had passed, he would have run it at home, as well, but that was where she had put her foot down. Now, a little over a year after her passing, he still couldn't bring himself to run it in the house. He felt that doing so would dishonor her, in a way. But he ran it in the truck, every chance he got. Mankind had mapped the human genome, and put a robot on Mars, but as far as Nagle was concerned, air conditioning was still humanity's greatest invention.

As they continued on their way, the vents blew directly onto McLeod in the center of the bench seat. It chilled his wet clothing, and a mile down the road he sneezed. He didn't get his hand up in time, and particles swirled through the cab.

What Nagle hadn't mentioned to Collins and McLeod was that he had just finished his second round of chemo at the VA Hospital for his prostate, leaving his immune system good and weak.

The virus pinwheeling through the cab hit him fast and hard.

During his time as a River Rat, Nagle had fought both the NVA and the Vietcong up and down South Vietnam's densely jungled Mekong River and its snakelike tributaries. He'd inspected junk boats, farming floats, and Sampans, looking for smuggled weapons and enemy combatants. He'd ferried US Army soldiers and Marines on missions. He'd survived numerous ambushes and firefights. Even now, all these years later, every gunshot that echoed across the fields and woods of rural Illinois during hunting season made him think of the twin fifty calibers and M60s he'd used once upon a time. He thought about the kids he'd killed, while he himself was just a kid, as well.

Often, he thought about one fight in particular. Their orders were to ambush a group of nearly a hundred Vietcong troops, who were making their way through the jungle under the cover of darkness, near the shore. Nagle and the other three men assigned to his boat, as well as their interpreter, reached the area and camouflaged their vessel. A second PBR craft arrived as backup, and did the same. When the enemy contingent emerged along the riverbank, both boats had opened fire with everything they had, bombarding the shoreline with the fifty calibers, M-79 grenade launchers, and M-60s. The rear of the enemy column fled into the jungle. At dawn, the rest lay dead, in and out of the water. It was only then that Nagle noticed the unexploded rocket propelled grenade lying on the deck beside him. A Vietcong soldier had fired it at him during the fight, but for whatever reason, it hadn't gone off. Nagle and the crew had to wait for a demolition expert to extract the ordinance.

In the decades since then, Nagle had often wished that he'd been allowed to bring the unexploded ordnance home with him—as a souvenir.

And as a reminder.

Richard Nagle had faced a lot in his life. He'd faced the Vietcong. He'd faced the cancer that claimed his wife.

But he'd never faced an enemy like White Fire.

5

"My God," Nagle gasped.

McLeod grunted through chattering teeth in apparent agreement.

Collins could only stare. The damage in Godfrey put the chaos they'd seen in the fields on the outskirts of town to shame. Collins had once visited a war-ravaged African community to help combat a flu outbreak; a village that the rebels had shelled for three days straight. The tornado had caused remarkably similar destruction in less than ten minutes.

Residents were already picking through the rubble or milling about aimlessly in the streets. One group of people in brightly colored ponchos prayed on a street corner in front of a church with broken windows. Fragments of stained glass littered the sidewalk at their feet. Another man calmly held a leash while his terrier did its business on a fallen tree. McLeod whistled, and Collins shook his head, but none of them said another word as Nagle navigated the rain swept streets. Both Collins and McLeod shivered, partly from shock and partly from the temperature inside the truck.

Nagle sighed, and Collins glanced at him. Some of the street signs were missing, and Collins hoped the old man wasn't lost.

"We okay, Mr. Nagle?"

"Oh, sure." The old man nodded. His expression was grim. "I just...it's hard, seeing the town like this. And wondering what's waiting for me at home. Can't wait to get

40

back there, but I'm kind of dreading it, too, if that makes any sense. I'm worried about my dog."

Collins felt a desperate pang of guilt. The old man wouldn't be returning home anytime soon.

Red and blue lights flashed atop a patrol car parked beneath a dead traffic light up ahead. A police officer stood in the intersection, using a pair of lighted batons to direct traffic.

"Can you drive up to him?" Collins asked.

Nagle nodded. "Sure thing, Captain."

The officer waved his batons as they approached. Nagle coasted to a stop, rolled down his window, and spat a stream of tobacco juice. Collins rolled down his window, as well.

"Excuse me," he called. "Has anyone established an emergency operations center yet?"

"Who wants to know?"

He held his credentials out the window. "Captain Tom Collins, US Army."

The officer placed a baton under one armpit and scowled as he examined the identification card. After a long pause, he handed it back to Collins and stepped back into the intersection. His expression was dumbfounded but happy.

"Well," he said. "The Army, huh? We'd be happy to have the help. The fire station's a mess, so they're setting up at the elementary school. The police chief and fire chief are already there, and I hear county and state personnel are on the way. Might want to touch base with them."

"Thanks." Collins turned to Nagle. "You know how to get there?"

The old man nodded. "Born and raised here. I'll probably die here, too."

He pulled into traffic at the officer's direction, narrowly avoiding a small dog that had apparently gotten lost from its owner during the storm. The poor creature's sodden fur dripped into its eyes. It stared at them forlornly.

The elementary school was a few blocks away at the southwest edge of town, and the tornado had mercifully bypassed this section of Godfrey. Were it not for the two fire engines they passed, and the cluster of emergency vehicles plastered with seals and logos gathered to one side of the lot, Collins could have almost believed the town had experienced just another rainy day.

A young firefighter in a blue t-shirt and cap flagged them down with his clipboard. "Can I help you, gentlemen?"

Collins flashed his identification again and quickly introduced himself.

"Army?" The young man appeared surprised. "You guys got here quick."

"I need to speak to whomever is in charge," Collins replied.

Sure." Nodding, the firefighter pointed to the nearby entrance. "That would be Chief Hansen. He's a big guy with a handlebar mustache. You can't miss him."

"Thanks." Collins climbed out of the truck and helped McLeod do the same.

"You fellas take care now," Nagle called.

Collins paused and turned. He pointed at the firefighter. "What's your name?"

"Chris. Chris Brannon."

Collins nodded at the truck. "Make sure he doesn't leave. It's a matter of national security. Understood?"

The firefighter glanced at Mr. Nagle, and then nodded. His demeanor was nervous.

"How's that?" Nagle's expression was one of surprise.

"We need you to stay here, Mr. Nagle. Just for a little while."

McLeod nodded. "It's important."

"But," the old man protested, "I've got to get on home— see if I *still* have a home. I helped you boys out Did my duty. But I've got other responsibilities."

"And we appreciate your help," Collins said. "Really. But you can't leave. That's an order."

"Well, what about my dog?"

"As I said, it's a matter of national security."

"He doesn't look like a terrorist to me," the firefighter observed, his tone doubtful.

"Keep him here," Collins repeated.

Nagle frowned. "This because of whatever it was you had inside that van?"

Neither Collins nor McLeod responded. Instead, they turned around and walked toward the entrance.

"Look here," Nagle shouted after them, "I helped you boys out. Gave you a ride. Did my duty as an American citizen! You ain't got no right to keep me here. I thought we had an understanding? I've got rights. This is still America, isn't it?"

"Um…" the young fireman stared in confusion.

Collins turned around.

"Well," Nagle asked, "isn't it still America?"

"It is," Collins replied. "And if the two of you still want it to be when the sun comes up tomorrow, then do what I tell you, and stay there. I'll be back out as quick as I can, and I'll explain everything then. For now, just follow my orders."

They turned and headed inside the building, before the two men could argue with them further.

"You could have backed me up a little more strongly back there," Collins complained.

"I'm in too much pain to frighten civilians," McLeod countered. "Let's find whoever is in charge, and then find me some ibuprofen. Or even better, and eighteen-year old bottle of scotch."

"We find that…you'll have to fight me for it."

The lobby inside the elementary school was packed with people. Some were in uniform and others wore plainclothes. Collins scanned the room, taking it all in. Someone had set up several foldout banquet tables, and they were piled with maps, paperwork, radios, a pair of laptop computers, and various medical gear. There was talk of cots, blankets, fresh water, and canned goods. They heard the word "insurance" at least twice.

McLeod pointed. "That must be him, right?"

A beefy, broad-shouldered man stood at the back of the crowd. Collins thought the mustache made him look like a gun-fighting bodybuilder.

"Yeah," Collins agreed. "That must be."

They made their way through the throng toward him.

"Excuse me," Collins began. "Are you Chief Hansen?"

The man glanced at him, and then did a double take when he spotted Collins' uniform. "Damn. You guys sure showed up fast. You even made it here before the media."

"I'm not sure who you expected, but I was already coming through town." Once again Collins introduced himself and showed his credentials. "This is Phil McLeod. He was riding with me."

McLeod fished his own identification out of his pocket, wincing as he did.

"How's that arm, Mr. McLeod?" Hansen asked.

"Bad as it looks," McLeod grunted, handing over his identification.

Hansen pinched it between his huge fingers and inspected it. "Private contractor?"

McLeod nodded. "Driving for the CDC."

"Centers for Disease Control? What's this about? Something tells me you fellas aren't here to volunteer your help with the storm clean-up."

"No." Collins lowered his voice. "Is there somewhere we can talk in private, Chief Hansen?"

Hansen stared at them. His Adam's apple bobbed. Then he turned and motioned for them to follow him. Collins walked behind him. McLeod lagged, his posture slumped as he trailed along. Hansen led them to a classroom and shut the door.

"This private enough?" Chief Hansen stood next to the chalkboard, eyeing them warily.

McLeod eased himself atop the teacher's desk, letting his legs dangle over the side. Collins remained standing.

"This will be fine," Collins said. "We appreciate it. Now, I must caution you…what I'm about to tell you is for your ears only.

Hansen rubbed his tired eyes. "I suspect I'm not going to like whatever it is."

"You're not wrong about that," McLeod wheezed.

6

Chris Brannon had finished his probationary period only two months before, and he enjoyed being a part of the Godfrey Fire Protection District. It was fun, it was rewarding, he liked the camaraderie, and it even got him out of work at the furniture plant from time to time.

At the moment, however, he wished he was out there helping survivors, clearing roads, and putting out fires rather than taking notes on a map and playing traffic director for the EMS services and first responders arriving for mutual aid. Chief Hansen said he wanted the "more experienced" men "out in the shit." And to add insult to injury, now the Army guy had him guarding this old man, Mr. Nagle.

Britney Scofield wandered by, holding a wet rag to a cut on her forehead. Chris had known her since middle school, and while they had never exactly been friends or run in the same social circles, their interactions were friendly enough when their paths crossed at the bar or in town. Chris thought that she looked good, despite the blood on her clothing. He watched her ass and sighed. Then he took a deep breath and called out.

"How you doing, Britney?"

She turned to him, her eyes glassy, and shrugged. "My apartment windows got blown out and a telephone pole landed on my car."

"Aw hell. I'm sorry to hear that. How's your head? Can I do anything for you?"

"No," she said, but the rest of her statement was drowned out as Mr. Nagle started his engine.

Chris jumped, startled. "Hey!"

Mr. Nagle began to back his truck out of the parking space.

"Whoa whoa whoa!" Chris held up his hand, palm out. "Just where in the hell do you think you're going?"

"Home!" Mr. Nagle scowled.

"Like hell you are. Turn this truck off! I was told to keep you here."

"And a fine job you're doing. That young woman's ass part of your orders, too?"

"Now look—"

"No, you look. Stay here and flirt with that girl if you want, but I need to see my house and check on my dog. He doesn't like to be left alone, and this storm probably spooked him."

Chris eyed the gold wedding band on the old man's ring finger.

"My wife's dead," Nagle added. "Cancer. I still wear the ring. You have a problem with that?"

"No, sir"

"Then move aside. My dog will be worried about me."

"I'll see you later, Chris," Britney called, waving.

"No!" He held up a hand. "Hang on a second."

Eyes wide, Britney Scofield hurried away. Chris sighed in exasperation.

"Get out of the way," Nagle warned.

"I said to turn this truck off, you old fart!"

"Don't try to tell me what to do," Nagle grumbled. "I was fighting overseas before you were even a gleam in your Daddy's eye."

"You heard what they said. I was asked to keep you here." Chris put his hand on the driver's side door handle. "Now, turn the truck off. We're both staying put."

"Yeah?" Mr. Nagle sneered. "What for? If he wants to pin a medal on me for giving him a ride, I don't need it."

Chris was close enough to feel the old man's breath on him. He caught a faint whiff of Copenhagen and black licorice. Disgusted, he backed away.

"I asked you a question," Mr. Nagle said, impatient. "What's he need with me?"

Chris shrugged. "You know better than me. What was it you asked him, about his van?"

Nagle lowered his voice. "They're working for the CDC."

"What's that?"

"The Center for goddamn Disease Control! How can you be a first responder and not know that?"

Chris shrugged. "So, what…they were carrying some kind of virus? Biological warfare stuff? Like Ebola or something?"

"He didn't say," Nagle admitted.

"Well, he did say we were supposed to stay here. I think it would be a good idea to listen to him."

"Or what?" Nagle challenged. "I got a right to look after my own."

"Sir, I—"

"You do what you gotta do. He'll find me if he needs me." Nagle revved the engine. "Now, for the last time, move aside. I don't want to run over your foot, but so help me God, I will."

Chris hopped back out of the way, exasperated. The passenger-side mirror missed his chest by inches as the old man backed across the lot, turned, and then drove away. Chris watched his taillights fade, and shook his head.

"Shit…"

His radio crackled at his side. Chris pulled it from his belt, and thumbed the button.

"Go ahead."

"Got a gas leak at 853 South Maple. Utility company is already on hand."

"Copy that," Chris replied. He clipped the radio back on his belt and consulted the map on his clipboard. Then he made a mark by the location. Finished, he glanced up again, hoping to catch sight of Britney, but she was gone.

Chris sighed. "It's going to be a long night."

But he was wrong.

Neither of them knew it, but Mr. Richard Nagle would be dead by midnight.

Chris Brannon would follow shortly after.

7

"Jesus Christ…" Chief Hansen crossed his arms and stared at the floor as he listened to the two men. "What kind of symptoms are we looking for?"

"High fevers," Collins replied. "Along with intense headaches, joint pains, and muscle spasms. As it progresses, paralysis. Victims usually asphyxiate.

"If their brains don't cook first," McLeod added.

"Jesus Christ," Hansen repeated. Beads of sweat dotted his forehead and nose. "What do we do about it? You gentlemen saw what happened outside. We're about to have possibly hundreds of people living in this gymnasium, probably for days, if not weeks!"

"Set up the classrooms as quarantine rooms." Collins kept his tone calm. "We'll have as much vaccine flown in as we can, and get you some more personnel."

"Alright," Hansen said. "Then I guess we best stop wasting time and get you guys some phones. I'll get someone to look at your arm, too, Mr. McLeod."

"Thank you," McLeod replied.

"Our first priority," Collins said, "is the old man who brought us into town, and your volunteer firefighter."

"Agreed." Hansen nodded. "I hope you're wrong about this. Chris is a good kid."

"That's the firefighter?" McLeod asked.

Hansen nodded. "Chris Brannon."

"One other thing." Collins grabbed Hansen at the classroom door. "This virus moves *fast*. And we were only just beginning to produce a vaccine, so there's not going to be much."

"What are you telling me, Captain Collins?"

"If this thing spreads..." Collins paused. He glanced at McLeod and then back to the chief. "A lot of people are going to die. The only protection against it is the vaccine. If a person contracts it before that..." He shrugged.

Hansen shook his head and ripped the door open. "Just fucking wonderful."

The chief set them both up with some emergency satellite phones. Then, a paramedic attended to McLeod, carefully unwrapping the bandage covering his injured arm. Confident he was being cared for, Collins excused himself and wandered the school building until he found a quiet area—a darkened hallway lined with children's artwork and safety posters. There, he powered up the emergency phone and took a deep, shuddering breath.

"Okay," he whispered. "Here we go."

His voice echoed faintly in the corridor. Collins placed a call back to his base, and got hold of a desk sergeant. He identified himself, gave a code for urgency, and asked to speak with Colonel Sharpe. The desk sergeant stuttered as he placed Collins on hold.

While he waited, Collins glanced at the artwork on the walls—crayon drawings from the children of Godfrey, detailing their houses and their families. Yellow crayon suns hung in blue crayon skies, shining down upon stick figure parents, stick figure children, and their stick figure pets. Everyone in the drawings seemed happy. None of them seemed sick. Swallowing hard, he glanced down at the tiled floor.

"This is Colonel Sharpe."

"Sir, this is Captain Collins."

"Tom? I take it this isn't a social call."

"No, sir. VM2 is loose. I repeat, White Fire is in the

wind. We may have an outbreak on our hands."

"*May* have an outbreak?"

"Affirmative."

"Sounds more like we probably *do* have an outbreak, to me. Are you calling from a secure line?"

"Negative, sir. But it's the only line I have available, currently."

"Understood. Okay, listen up, Captain."

The Colonel didn't ask what had happened, and Collins didn't offer details. Both men knew the drill. Both men new that time was of the utmost importance. How the virus had been released didn't matter. The only thing that mattered now was containment. Their conversation took only three minutes. When they were finished, Collins disconnected the call and took another shuddering breath. He collected himself and then walked back down the hallway, rejoining the others.

"Help is on the way," he told Hansen and McLeod.

The chief nodded, but before he could reply, a first responder hurried over to him with a question.

Collins turned to McLeod. "They fix you up?"

He turned, displaying fresh bandages. "I'll be okay. Should we see to Mr. Nagle and Chief Hansen's man?"

Collins nodded.

The two men walked toward the exit. After a moment, Chief Hansen disengaged himself from the command center and hurried along behind them. The glass doors slid open.

"Does this building still have electricity?" McLeod asked.

"No," Hansen replied. "We're running on generators. What's the chances the army will bring us some extra—"

"Where the hell is he?" Collins stopped in his tracks on the sidewalk, and pointed at the now empty spot along the curb where Nagle's truck had been parked. He snapped his fingers at the young firefighter. "Hey, what's your name again?"

"C-chris. Chris Brannon."

Collins ran over to him. McLeod and Hansen rushed after him. Chris took a faltering step backward, his eyes wide.

"I told you to keep that old man here!"

"He wanted to go home," Chris stammered. "He wanted to see if his house was damaged. He kept going on and on about his damned dog. What was I supposed to do?"

"Jesus Christ...You have *no idea* what you've just done!"

"Then maybe you should have warned him," Chief Hansen growled. "This is your cluster-fuck, Captain Collins. You want to be pissed off, that's fine, but you take it out on somebody other than my men."

A vein in Collins's forehead twitched. His hands clenched into fists.

McLeod reached out and squeezed Collins's shoulder. "Easy, Tom."

Chief Hansen stepped forward and addressed the young firefighter. "Chris, I want you to go get your respirator out of my truck. We'll be telling everyone else to do the same over the radio. If anyone comes back here not wearing their mask, send them to me immediately."

"Yes, sir." The kid glanced at Collins and McLeod and then trotted over to a large Chevy Suburban parked near the sidewalk.

Collins paced back and forth, his hands on his hips. He was rapidly losing control of the situation. They needed roadblocks and quarantines, fast. If he ever got his hands on the jokers running weather data...

Hansen cleared his throat. "I'd appreciate it if you didn't yell at my people, Captain. This situation is already tough and stressful for them."

"Tough and stressful?" Collins turned on the larger man. "That old man may have been infected. I told your people to keep him here!"

"Did you get the old man's name?" Hansen asked.

53

"Yes. It's Richard Nagle."

Chief Hansen frowned. "I don't know him. We'll have to see if he's listed."

"We wouldn't have to," Collins spat, "if your man had kept him here like I told him to."

Hansen leaned closer. "Did you warn him of the trouble? Did you tell him to stay put yourself? Did you bring him into the school with you?"

Collins glared.

"I didn't think so. Now, you listen to me, Captain Collins. I understand the gravity of your situation. But look around you. In case you didn't notice, we just got ass-fucked by a tornado. My people have a lot on their minds right now, even without the happy fucking news you just delivered. Fighting each other isn't going to improve our situation."

"Agreed," McLeod said. "How about you, Tom?"

"Okay," Collins admitted. "I'm sorry if I was out of line. But this situation is dire, and time is of the essence."

The young firefighter, Chris, returned, wearing a mask over his mouth and nose. The respirator looked too big for his face. In any other circumstances, it would have been almost comical.

Collins turned back to the Chief. "Nagle. We need to find him. Fast."

"We'll do what we can, but you need to understand that we've already got our hands full helping the injured, putting out fires, dealing with gas leaks, and searching for survivors."

"Maybe I didn't make myself clear, Chief."

Chief Hansen stared at the ground. "You did. We'll make it a priority."

"Fine. We also need to talk about roadblocks."

"Let me ask you something first. And you be straight with me."

"Sure. If I can."

"Are we going to be safe with just these little respirators?"

Collins opened his mouth to respond, but then he paused. He looked at the respirator Chris Brannon wore. It was little more than a glorified painter's mask with a few extra filters on it. Depending on the density of the filters, it might block the virus. But if it settled on someone's hand, and they wiped their eyes or ate without washing first, it would easily make the transition to their bloodstream.

"I hope so."

"You *hope* so?"

"You asked me to be straight with you, Chief. Well, that's as honest as I can be. I hope they'll be enough, but the truth is, I don't know."

Hansen opened his mouth to respond, but before he could, McLeod began to cough.

8

A weaponized virus is a double-edged sword.

It spreads quickly and attacks hard, which is exactly the effect one wants to achieve in a warfare situation. However, it does the same thing during an accidental release.

Word got around town that the school gym was being turned into a shelter. People trickled in at first, mostly seeking medical assistance, electricity, or a wi-fi signal. One man told a neighbor he'd best get his family over to the gym while there were still enough free bunks, and as that thought passed through the rumor mill, it became "there's not enough room for everyone at the shelter."

The trickle became a flood. The firefighters handled the traffic well, and there was little jostling and fighting amongst the people as they secured their own little section of flooring.

The virus thrived.

The media arrived before the National Guard or the American Red Cross. The reporters and camera crews made their way through the crowd and coached soundbite-friendly answers from the people of Godfrey. Reporters shook their hands and came away infected, then returned to their vans to survey the carnage and make their reports. They talked to more people who attempted to turn their damaged homes into shelters, or awaited the arrival of their insurance agent. People breathed into microphones, which then became deadlier than a loaded gun. They shared bottles of water, passing them around and sipping together, their mouths touching the deadly plastic rims.

The virus spread.

The first insurance agent on the scene actually arrived with a briefcase full of cash. He had his customers sign a receipt, and then handed them enough money to get a hotel room for the night, as well as clothing and food. The stacks of paper bills crawled with the virus, as did the pen he handed them to sign the receipt with.

The local National Guard unit activated. It took time to reach many of the soldiers, and still more time for them to arrive and assemble. It was near dusk when they reached Godfrey. By then, the rain had picked up again, although sporadically. The Guardsmen had orders to blockade the town, and that's what they did, enacting a total quarantine. A number of people who had planned on leaving town to stay with family or find hotels found themselves trapped in Godfrey instead.

The virus was trapped inside with them.

9

The rain had ended, but the sky was still dark and ominous when the choppers set down in the football field behind the school. Collins held his cap to his head and jogged toward them. The rotors whirred, and the hydraulics whined. Men in bio-suits hurriedly debarked from the helicopters and carried their gear to the school. Their movements were efficient and orderly. Collins saluted when he saw Colonel Sharpe striding across the field.

"As you were, Captain," Sharpe shouted over the spinning props. "No time for pleasantries. Give me a sit rep."

Collins quickly told him about the roadblocks and the setup inside the school, as well as the quarantine arrangements.

Frowning, Sharpe folded his hands behind his back. "Has anyone left town?"

"Unknown, sir," Collins said.

"Okay, Captain. Fair enough, given the fluidity of the situation. We're going to need to get the word out to area clinics and hospitals. We're not playing the classified game any longer."

"Sir?"

"You heard me. There's no time for secrecy. Secrecy will only make matters worse. I want all medical personnel in on this. They are our best defense. They don't need to know the details, but they need to know what they're dealing with. Understood?"

"Copy that."

"If we get outbreaks anywhere else, I want to know about

it immediately. Are we clear?"

"Crystal, sir. And what about the press?"

"They don't need to know anything yet. While I want all emergency responders briefed, we can still maintain secrecy with the media a little while longer. Let's get a handle on the situation here before we start spreading panic. Do we have anyone with symptoms yet?"

"No, sir."

"Good." Sharpe smiled. "Who knows? Maybe we'll get lucky, and this will all blow over before we have to worry about it."

Collins doubted it, but he held his tongue. He led Sharpe forward. Chief Hansen waited for them at the fringe of the field, and Collins introduced the two men to each other. Hansen dwarfed the bookish Colonel, even given the few inches the bio-suit added to Sharpe's height.

"Will you be taking over, Colonel?" Hansen asked Sharpe.

"No, this is still your ballgame, Chief. We're only here to advise and contain, and help where we can. We've got about a hundred doses of vaccine, and we'd like to start by administering it to emergency personnel, so that they can keep doing their job without spreading the virus."

"It would help if I knew fully what we're dealing with, Colonel."

"I understand that, and further, I sympathize. I just informed Captain Collins that we needed to clue you in. While the specifics must remain classified, I can tell you that it's a weaponized strain of viral meningitis. It's fast and it's deadly."

"Ours?"

"We didn't manufacture it, no. Our sample came from a foreign nation. That's all I can say."

"Good enough," Hansen said. "I understand. Can't violate national security."

"Exactly," Sharpe told him. "And I appreciate your understanding. Oh, and one more thing, Chief. Keep an eye on everyone you administer the vaccine to. The vaccine itself is not deadly, but it may cause nausea or low fevers."

"Are you shitting me?"

"It's not designed for perfection, Chief. Its purpose is just to keep our boys fighting when administered in the field. Soldiers can still fight when puking. They've done it in every war since the dawn of humankind."

A technician, clad in a bio-suit, called for Sharpe's attention. The Colonel excused himself and walked away.

Hansen glared at Collins. "You people are just full of good fucking news."

"I'm sorry, Chief. I really am. Meanwhile, any word on Mr. Nagle?"

"I sent someone over to his house, but it was locked up tight and no answer when they knocked. No lights on, either."

"Well, of course there wouldn't be, Collins reasoned. "The power is out."

"I mean candlelight. Lanterns. There was no indication he was there."

"Was his truck parked outside?"

Hansen flinched. "I don't know."

"Jesus fucking Christ...do I need to go check on him myself?"

"I'll have someone handle it," Hansen insisted. "Just do me a favor, will you? Next time you and McLeod decide to take Ebola or cholera out for a nice, leisurely Sunday drive, stay the fuck away from my town!"

Collins watched Hansen stomp off toward the front of the school. He couldn't blame the man for being pissed off. He would be, too, if their roles were reversed. Fortunately, from what he'd seen of the man so far, the chief was all business rather than the type to focus on laying blame. He seemed the type who was more concerned about controlling the situation than trying to figure out whom to throw under the media and political buses.

Wincing, Collins pinched the bridge of his nose. A headache was beginning to form behind his eyes. His toe, while no longer throbbing, still hurt, and every time he breathed through his mouth, he felt a sharp pain on his tooth. He thought about tracking down some water and ibuprofen, but then a thought occurred to him. What if his headache was the first sign of VM2 infection? What if he'd contracted White Fire? He smacked his lips. His mouth had suddenly gone dry.

No. That was impossible. He'd been vaccinated. Everybody in his unit had been. He didn't have the disease. He decided that he was just dehydrated, and perhaps suffering from slight shock. Resolving to find a bottle of water, Collins stalked back into the school. He spotted McLeod in the hallway, sitting in a chair beneath an educational fire safety poster with a cartoon bear dressed like a forest ranger.

"How are you feeling?" Collins asked, approaching.

"Like shit," McLeod grunted. "Although the painkillers are starting to kick in. You?"

"Headache."

McLeod's eyes widened. "You think...?"

Collins shook his head. "I'm just thirsty, is all. Dehydrated."

McLeod turned his attention back to the bustling personnel all around them. "So, what now?"

"You know the drill."

"No, I mean what now for us, Tom? They don't seem to have any use for us at this point."

"I guess we wait for orders. Sharpe is here. Once he gets a handle on things, I'm sure they'll have something for us to do. Sit tight until then."

"Hurry up and wait, huh?"

"Some things never change."

McLeod grinned, but Collins thought it was a sad expression.

"Oh, how I wish that were true, Tom. Do you know…I'm the only gay person I know of who listens to Rush?"

Collins blinked. "You mean the talk show host?"

McLeod rolled his eyes. "No, not Rush Limbaugh. Fuck that guy. I'm talking about the band. You know? Rush!"

"The band whose lead singer sounds like a drowning bag of cats?"

"Heathen."

"I was never a fan. Although, I guessed I like that Tom Sawyer song."

"That was one of their big hits, for sure. And that's the one I was thinking of, actually. In that song, they sing that changes aren't permanent, but that change is."

"I'm not following you, Phil."

"I'm thinking about me and Toby. Things changed between us, but I never thought they would. Never thought I'd enlist. Never thought I'd become a civilian Never thought I'd partner up with you. Never thought I'd end up dying in a little town in the middle of Illinois."

"Nobody is dying, Phil."

"You sure about that?"

Collins gestured at the activity around them. "They all seem pretty healthy, right? Nobody dying here."

McLeod shrugged. "Give it another few hours, and see if that changes."

***

True to his word, Colonel Sharpe let Chief Hansen direct his men. The bio-suited soldiers administered vaccine shots to the emergency crews as they came and went, and a few more doses to people in the gymnasium to prevent—or at least slow—the spread of the virus. As expected, there were lots of questions and more than a little concern over the sudden appearance of the soldiers, and an emergency worker slipped word to a friend of his that he'd heard that Collins and McLeod were with the CDC. The destruction from the tornado was forgotten in the face of this news. The Center for Disease Control didn't show up for simple storm recovery efforts.

When it became evident that rumors were spreading, Sharpe told the citizens gathered in the gym that there was an accident with a virus sample and assured them that the military presence was merely a precaution. Things would be back to normal in no time at all. Chief Hansen backed him up, and it seemed to appease the people to hear a local making the same promises.

Once the Godfrey residents knew the situation, it became much harder to keep it from the press. Colonel Sharpe reluctantly found himself making an official statement at a hastily-arranged news conference, and he stuck to his "precautionary measures" story. He advised relief workers en route to Godfrey to bring respirators, and advised Godfrey citizens to stay indoors when possible, or come to the gym for shelter. He asked that citizens not leave town for twenty-four hours to ensure they were not infected. When the press pushed back on this, he admitted that, in fact, the residents couldn't leave town, due to the blockade. Nor could the reporters themselves. After that, some among the press corps began to make the news about themselves, rather than the townspeople.

The story became breaking news on all three of the cable news networks, and that got the politicians involved. Most of them wanted to know what their offices could do to help. A few started looking into ways to use this against their political opponents. Both would have their hands full over the next several days.

***

The virus manifested in its first victim at 6:33pm that evening. He had been sweating profusely for some time, and a slight headache had started at the base of his skull, yet he hadn't recognized the symptoms for what they were, chalking them up instead to just stress or the injuries he'd suffered during the tornado. The headache built up swiftly, and soon his temperature spiked.

With mounting terror, the man finally recognized the symptoms and called for help immediately.

His name was Phil McLeod.

10

"Temperature one oh three point five," a paramedic called. "Where are those antibiotics? I need them!"

McLeod reached for Collins with one trembling, sweaty hand. His red-rimmed eyes were wide and pleading. Collins took his hand and squeezed. Then he patted McLeod's head. His hair was slick with perspiration.

"Hang in there, Phil." His tongue felt thick in his mouth. "We're working on it."

"But...the vaccine..." McLeod whispered.

"You must already have been infected."

"You're...not sick..."

"I was vaccinated two weeks ago."

McLeod's eyes widened even farther. "But...why not...?"

"You're a civilian, Phil. I'm not. We couldn't risk it. I'm sorry. I really am."

McLeod's face screwed up angrily, then he groaned and winced. Bloody phlegm and saliva leaked from the corner of his mouth.

"F...fuck...you...Tom..."

His eyes rolled into the back of his head and he relaxed onto the stretcher.

"Get him on that chopper!" Collins snapped. "Go, go, go goddamn it!"

The paramedics rushed him toward the door. EMTs and volunteers scrambled to get out of their way. A small group of civilians looked on in wide-eyed terror. One woman crossed herself. Collins spotted Chief Hansen, clutching a clipboard piled with paperwork, and conferring with two firefighters.

"Chief!"

The big man glanced up.

"Make sure they isolate him," Collins shouted, gesturing at McLeod's stretcher. "Tell them they'll need to start a spinal tap *immediately!*"

Frowning, Hansen crossed the room and pulled Collins aside.

"They know how to do their goddamn jobs," he said, keeping his voice low "So, how about you lay off them?"

"Sorry." Collins deflated. He took off his cap, rubbed his head, and plopped it back on. "You're right. I'm sorry. It's just...I feel like it's my fault, you know? I can't let him die. He's an old friend."

Chief Hansen's tone softened. "Try not to worry. He's in good hands. We've dealt with meningitis before."

Collins shook his head. "Not like this you haven't."

Hansen's demeanor changed again. He slammed his paperwork to the table. "You think I don't know that? I have to go with what you people are giving me, which isn't a whole hell of a lot!"

"Well, in that case, how about I—"

"That's enough, gentlemen."

Collins hadn't been aware of Colonel Sharpe approaching. The officer seemed to materialize out of nowhere. He insinuated himself between the two of them, and glowered up at Hansen.

"You don't need to know the virus's history to fight it, Chief Hansen. Your people know the symptoms, they know the treatment, and we're delivering the supplies. If you can't handle it, Chief Hansen, then I'll relieve you of your command."

The big man scowled down at the smaller officer.

"I thought you said this was still my ballgame, Colonel? That you were only here to advise and contain, and help?"

"That's affirmative, Chief," Sharpe replied. "It is still

your ballgame. So, how about you get with the team and play ball?"

Hansen glared at them both for a moment, then nodded curtly and turned back to his business.

Sharpe pursed his thin lips. "Captain, I need a word."

Collins stepped to a quiet corner with the Colonel. "Yes, sir?"

"Do you need a break, Tom?"

"No, sir, I'm fine."

"Are you sure? I really need you to stay frosty, here. You've been through a lot and I'll understand if you need a quick break. McLeod was your friend. You and he go back a long way, I'm told."

Collins nodded. "We do."

"You're aware of what will most likely happen to him." Sharpe's tone indicated a statement rather than a question.

"I am." Collins sighed, and shook his head. "He had a partner—a guy named Toby. They'd broken up recently, but someone should still inform him."

"When this is over," Sharpe replied. "Once we have full control."

Collins stared into the Colonel's eyes, unblinking. "And do you really think that will happen, sir?"

"I do. We've got roadblocks in place, and we're enforcing the quarantine. Nobody is getting in or out of this town. So far, we've been able to keep the press under control. We have a real chance here to stay on top of this thing. And that's why I need you to get your head in the game. Hansen may be gruff, but from what I've seen so far, he's a good man. More importantly, we need him, Tom. Without their cooperation, there's no way we'll contain this. I need you to play ball with him. Can you do that?"

Collins nodded again. "I can, sir. I think I just need to stay busy. I need a job."

A scream erupted from the gymnasium. Everyone

dropped what they were doing and ran to investigate. Collins and Sharpe pushed to the front of the crowd. A middle-aged woman had collapsed and now convulsed on the free throw line, the back of her head and her heels banging out a staccato beat on the floor. Two EMTs rushed to her side while a third gently ushered two other people—presumably her husband and daughter—back to the rest of the crowd.

"Here we go," Sharpe muttered. "You wanted something to occupy your time, Tom? You got your wish."

Collins closed his eyes and tried not to weep. He thought of Cheryl, and their kids. He suddenly wanted to call them. He could deal with the usual incriminations, the usual accusations and animosity that such contact brought. All the drama would be worth it, if only to hear their voices for a brief moment.

Instead, he went to work.

He was unaware that he was crying until a paramedic sheepishly pointed it out to him.

***

Phil McLeod died at 11:01pm. A grim-faced Chief Hansen informed him of the news at 11:15, but by then, Collins had his hands full with other victims. There was no time to grieve for his friend.

The virus raged

11

By midnight, they had forty-two more cases of VM2 in the gym alone. Sixteen more arrived from around the town. Collins performed six spinal taps himself, a tricky procedure even in clean hospital conditions. The helicopters slowly ferried them to neighboring hospitals, but three cases already showed up at one of them and they grew concerned about overcrowding.

"The spiders," the woman Collins worked on cried. "Get them off me. They've got faces like human babies. Oh God, get them off!"

She clawed at her arms and chest and ripped the antibiotic drip out of her arm.

"Damn it!" Collins pinned her shoulders to the cot. "Stay still, ma'am."

"But the spiders! Can't you hear what they're whispering?"

"I need you to stay still," Collins urged. "There are no spiders!"

Her red-rimmed eyes locked on his, and her chest heaved beneath him. Heat roiled off her in waves, and she stank of sour sweat.

"You're hallucinating," he continued. "Do you understand me? There are no spiders."

She nodded vigorously, her forehead slick and shiny with perspiration.

"Say it with me. There are no spiders."

"N-no s-spiders…" Her tone was doubtful.

"You're just feeling sweat. It's not spiders. Just your sweat on your skin. I need you to calm down, so I can put the IV back in. Can you do that for me?"

She relaxed. "Y-yes. I'm sorry."

An Army medic appeared and loomed over at them. Collins nodded at him, and then turned back to the woman. She stared at the medic's bio-suit in horror.

"It's okay," Collins assured her. "It's standard orders for him to be wearing that. You don't see me wearing one, right?"

She nodded, and choked down a sob.

"I'm going to let go of you now," he said. "Please, stay still."

Collins eased up, and she turned her left arm toward him. She wiped sweat from her forehead with her right, and then covered her eyes as she cried.

"I know it hurts, Collins soothed. "Just let the medicine do its work and we'll get you through this, okay?"

"Okay." She jerked but did not resist when he slid the IV needle back in. The medic handed him a length of surgical tape, and Collins wrapped it around her arm to secure the needle.

"Take it from here, okay?" Collins placed his hand on the medic's shoulder as he stood. The man's bio-suit crinkled noisily.

"Yes, sir."

In his mind, Collins saw McLeod's eyes, and the recrimination in them. His hands trembled as he wiped the sweat on his pants. *Now* he needed that break. The generator kept the lights on, and the equipment working, but what they really needed was to get the air conditioner going, for both the patients' and the doctors' sakes. The heat from all those bodies in all those rooms built up quick.

Collins weaved, stumbling a bit as he maneuvered across the gymnasium. He spotted Colonel Sharpe barking orders into a radio, and Chief Hansen gulping down a bottle of water. The big man looked as exhausted as Collins felt. He considered walking over and attempting to make piece—perhaps seeing if the Chief wanted to take a break with him. Before he could, however, Hansen drained the bottle, tossed it into a recycling bin, and wandered back into the fray. Shaking his head, Collins pushed through the double doors.

The hallway was cooler, though only slightly so. He leaned against the bare corkboard on the wall for a moment and let the sweat evaporate from his cheeks and forehead. It felt good to take some of the weight off his lower back and legs. He stared at the announcements and posters adorning the wall across from him, and thought about the children of Godfrey. How long has this place—this school—served them? Now, it was something very different. The halls and classrooms had once rung with laughter and learning, songs and the sounds of play. When the school reopened—*if* it reopened—would the screams and moans of the sick and dying echo down these corridors instead? Was it possible for a traumatic event to spawn a ghost—not of a victim, but of the event itself?

Jesus, he thought. *Get a grip on yourself, Tom. You don't believe in ghosts...*

Collins remembered the discussion he'd been having with McLeod, back in the van—their talk about religion and the afterlife. Now, Phil was dead. Had he gotten an answer? Had McLeod found out if there was an afterlife, after all?

Collins still didn't believe in one.

But he desperately wanted to.

His thoughts turned to Cheryl and the kids again. Then to his aching tooth. Another muffled scream echoed from the gym, followed by a tremendous clamor. It sounded like somebody had knocked over a tray of medical instruments, perhaps.

Collins closed his eyes and let a deep calm overtake him. Just for a minute, he told himself. Just a quick moment of rest and he'd have his second wind.

Just for a minute...

His head drooped, and his chin bounced off his chest. He woke with a start and pushed off the wall. The hall echoed again with the muted groans of feverish patients. Collins pressed his palms against his ears. He couldn't take the sound.

He decided to go outside. A breath of fresh air would probably do him good. Maybe he'd grab a quick bite to eat, as well, before returning to work. The water fountain down the hall caught his eye and he walked over for a drink. He had visions of the water fountain at his elementary school. The water pressure had been minimal, and as kids, they had to wrap their lips around the spigot, tasting whatever germs the child who had used it before them had. This water fountain worked much better. The pressure was strong, and the water was cool and refreshing. Collins swallowed several gulps before grabbing a handful and splashing it across his face. Then he stood back, gasping. He shook his head and blinked water from his eyes.

The classroom door opened behind him, and through the blur of water he saw someone in a white lab coat step into the hallway. It occurred to him that none of the personnel on the site wore lab coats. Colonel Sharpe's troops all wore biohazard suits or fatigues. Chief Hansen's people wore their uniforms. And he didn't recall seeing a civilian in a lab coat, either.

Collins balled his fists and finished wiping the water from his eyes. His vision cleared, and his stomach lurched.

What he'd mistaken for a lab coat was actually a pale trench coat—one he'd seen before.

The man wearing it was familiar, as well.

Collins held up a hand. "Hey!"

The man grinned. "Hey, yourself."

"What are you do—"

The man ran for the door at the end of the hall. The trench

coat billowed out behind him like a cape. Collins shouted as he gave chase. The man sprinted like an Olympic runner. Collins hardly took six steps before the man reached the door and blasted through it. His long, white hair flowed out behind him, much like his attire. Collins noticed that although his own footsteps echoed in the corridor. the man's feet made no noise as he fled. No echoes. No pounding footfalls. It was as if he ran above the ground, on the air itself.

By the time Collins got to the door, the man had fled, and there was no sign of him. Collins burst through to the outside, and glanced around hurriedly. They'd come out behind the school. The rear parking lot was surprisingly empty of cars. Only a few emergency vehicles occupied the spaces. Collins assumed that the townspeople must have walked. Collins checked under those, and behind the big green garbage dumpsters, but there was no sign of the mysterious stranger. The neighboring field was wide open, and empty, as well— at least, as far as he could see in the overcast gloom.

"Shit."

He rested his hand on his pistol and looked around one more time before going inside. It had to be the same man he'd seen right before the tornado hit the van. He hadn't gotten a good look at his face, but he had the same white hair. It was the same guy. He was sure of it. Seeing him then and seeing him now couldn't be a coincidence. But what could he want? What was he doing here? Could he be a thrill seeker, first chasing the storm and now witnessing the effects of the virus first-hand? Or maybe he was a reporter sniffing out a deeper angle on the official story?

Regardless of who he was or what his intentions were, the man had to be found. If he was this close to the victims, he could be carrying the virus back to other people. And if the virus got out of Godfrey, they were all in serious trouble.

Collins ran back through the school to find Colonel Sharpe and a radio.

12

Richard Nagle arrived safely at home earlier that evening, and was pleased to find that his house had only been slightly damaged in the storm. More importantly, his dog was safe and sound, if somewhat frightened. Nagle curled up with the dog in the recliner, and petted him softly. He sat there for a long time, mulling over the events of the day, and his encounter with Collins and McLeod.

He stared at his wife's picture on the mantle. He missed her dearly—and every day. But at that moment, he missed her with an intensity he hadn't felt since the immediate days after her death. The grief was overwhelming, and he sat there in the dark, his tears spattering down onto the dog, his trembling fingers gripping the animal's fur.

Headlights flashed outside, followed by a knock at the door. Nagle choked on a sob and didn't answer. The caller knocked again. Then, after a few moments, the headlights faded, leaving him alone again.

When the headache struck, he went up to bed to lie down for a bit. The dog lay at the foot of the bed and whined. Nagle reached down with one hand and scratched the dog's head until the steady drip in his attic soothed them both to sleep. Over the next several hours, the heat of Nagle's fever poached his brain like an egg while the buildup of spinal fluid at the base of his skull squeezed his medulla like a grape. Mercifully, he remained unconscious through it all, until he died at 11:37pm.

A police officer would find his body a week later. The dog

hadn't eaten much of him yet. After an autopsy, the coroner would declare him the first official victim of the virus.

Until that time, the first victim (after McLeod) was thought to be Chris Brannon, the young firefighter. He died in the parking lot at 11:56pm, still clutching his respirator. A real estate agent named Helen Sanders followed. She died at 1:48am in Room 103, where the second graders would go to class if the school board could convince the town to reopen the school on time. Her husband held her hand and kissed her forehead through his breathing mask. Next was Ben Johnson, president of the High School's drama club, at 2:30am on the nose.

By dawn, the military doctors counted one hundred and eighty-three known sick in the school and the three nearest hospitals.

And the virus continued to spread.

13

Collins provided a description of the man in the pale overcoat, as well as a description of his Jeep to the National Guardsmen watching the perimeters of Godfrey. After two hours had passed with no results and no sign of either, Colonel Sharpe excused Collins from his current duties with the infected, so that he could personally lead the search.

"There's nothing more you can do here," Sharpe said. "And you're the only one who really knows what this guy looks like."

The two men stood outside the school, near a cluster of neatly trimmed shrubs, away from the bustling activity.

"Permission to speak freely, sir?"

Sharpe nodded. "Go ahead. What's on your mind?"

"Is this some kind of punishment...for arguing with Hansen, or for wrecking in the first place? Are you just getting me out of the way?"

"For Christ's sake, Tom..."

"Well, my apologies, Colonel, but that's what it feels like."

"Listen up, Captain Collins. If I wanted you out of the way, I'd just have the MPs arrest you. The fact is, I don't trust your mystery man's motives, either. Whether he was being nosy or malicious, the only way to know for sure is to find him, bring him in, and question him. At the very least, we need to make sure he doesn't breach the quarantine. You're the man for the job. So go do it."

Collins nodded. "Understood, sir. Thank you."

A police officer wearing thick rubber gloves and a

respirator trotted over to them.

"Excuse me," he said, "which one of you is Collins?"

"I'm Captain Collins."

Sharpe gave his shoulder a quick squeeze. "Good luck, Tom."

As the Colonel returned to his duties, the police officer appraised Collins.

"How can I help you, Officer...?"

"Huyck. Can you follow me? Chief Hansen sent me to find you. You're the one heading up the search for the guy in the Jeep, correct?"

Collins nodded. "Affirmative. Where's the Chief?"

"Washing blood of his hands."

Collins stumbled. "Is he hurt?"

"No. The retarded kid who used to bag groceries at the market just coughed up blood all him. Luckily, the Chief was wearing protective gear."

Collins didn't respond.

The cop led him to the first row of the parking lot, and laid a map over the hood of his cruiser. The thick rubber gloves covering his fingers caused him some difficulty with this task. Collins waited patiently, running his tongue over his missing crown. When the paper was unfolded, Huyck turned on a flashlight and pointed it at the map. A grid divided the city into sectors, and several notes had been jotted in most of the squares.

"We've been watching for your guy for some time now," Huyck said. "Some of these zones have been covered three times now—by your people, and the National Guard, and ours. So far there's no sign of a green Jeep."

"He's got to be here somewhere. Let's make sure we're covering the undamaged part of town, too. There's bound to be less commotion there, making it easier to hide."

"Begging your pardon, Captain, but if he's driving a Jeep, he could be long gone by now. A Wrangler could easily get out through the trees here or here and avoid the perimeter checks altogether." He pointed to the wooded areas on the map on the east and west side of town. The patch to the west appeared to be a park of some kind, and the trails wound through the hills and forest for miles before rejoining a highway on the opposite side.

"No." Collins frowned. "If he's ballsy enough to come into the school, he's not going anywhere. He'll want to keep an eye on things. I'm going to shift some of our people here, and put a few on foot." He made a wide circle around the school with his index finger. "Make sure your people know about it. We don't need someone mistaking us for prowlers or looters."

"Aye aye, Captain."

Huyck turned away and spoke into the microphone on his shoulder. Collins swallowed down his anger. The cop's tone had been thick with disdain. Obviously, he disagreed, but Collins ignored the urge to reprimand him, and let it go. The man was a civilian, not a soldier. This was his town. The people inside the school were people he knew. He had a right to be on edge.

It only took a few minutes to remobilize the National Guardsmen, and Collins ordered a young female private to find him a Humvee and another map of the town. She nodded, saluted, and hurried off. While he waited for her to return, Collins stared up at the sky. It was pitch black, with no stars or moon. That would make the hunt much more difficult. As he stood there, mulling it over, the young woman returned and pulled alongside the curb. Collins jumped into the passenger side of the idling Humvee, and they sped off into the dark.

"What's your name, Private?"

"Gabriel, sir. Cara Gabriel."

"I'm Captain Collins. I want you to drive slow. Understood?"

She nodded.

Collins rummaged around in the cab, and found a night vision scope. He used it to get a good look between the houses. The top and sides of the Humvee had been taken off, giving him a good view all around.

With the exception of the power blackout, it appeared as if nothing had happened to the few blocks surrounding the school. Damage from the tornado was minimal. Leaves and small branches lay in yards and on the street, but there was no apocalyptic damage like the rest of Godfrey had suffered. Candles burned in many of the windows, and occasionally a dog barked at the soldiers and emergency personnel traipsing through the yards, but otherwise it was quiet.

Collins ordered Gabriel to widen the circle a bit, taking them into the path of the tornado. The hum of generators filled the air, and in a few places, people were already working beneath construction lights. Most of them wore respirators, making their expressions unreadable as they stopped what they were doing and turned to watch the Humvee go by.

What a mess, Collins thought. The cost of the physical damage alone was going to be astronomical. He couldn't begin to imagine what the medical costs would look like. The insurance companies were probably circling the wagons and trying to pass as much of it as possible on to the military or the government.

Gabriel brought the Humvee to a sudden halt. At first, Collins thought perhaps she'd spotted the Jeep, but then he realized what was wrong. The red, wet carcass of a cow lay splattered across the road in front of them.

"Drive over it," Collins said.

"Sir?"

"It's okay. It's not like the cow is going to feel it."

The front tired bumped up over the carcass, and Collins felt his stomach lurch along with their vehicle. He glanced at Gabriel, but the young woman's expression was stoic. The

Humvee jolted again as the rear tires went up and over the gory speed bump.

The tents of a Red Cross camp sprawled across the yards on one street. On the near edge, a woman tearfully thanked a pair of volunteers for the jars of baby formula they handed her. An infant squalled in her arms. The aroma of chicken soup filled the air. It touched—and surprised—Collins that the volunteers had showed up at all with the virus running loose. They were no doubt warned prior to their arrival, yet they had come anyway. It was a remarkable display of dedication. Of course, filth and disease were part of the game at many of the places these people visited. Maybe this was just par for the course.

Not everyone was in a giving mood. Collins listened to two calls on the police scanner. Police first arrested a young boy for boosting stereos out of disabled vehicles. In the background, the kid whined about the insurance covering it all anyway. The second was for a man who used a shotgun to warn everyone away from his house. He was apparently terrified of getting sick. Fortunately, nobody was hurt when they arrested him.

Collins was thankful this occurred in a sleepy little rural town. Things would be far, far worse in the city.

Speaking of sleepy, he thought as he covered a yawn with his palm. He leaned his head to his shoulders to stretch his neck, and wondered if those Red Cross folks had some coffee. By his watch it was nearly three in the morning.

"You doing okay, Private Gabriel?" he asked.

"Yes, sir."

"Where you from?"

"Washburn, sir."

"And where is that?"

"About thirty miles east of here, sir."

"Married?"

"Yes, sir. Four years now."

"And what does your husband, do?"

"He's an HVAC technician."

"Kids?"

The young soldier visibly brightened. "One son. Philip. He's three."

Collins turned his head away from the soldier and stifled a grimace. Maybe he shouldn't have asked. Not only did the boy's name remind him of McLeod, but he worried that the soldier might get sick, too. Poor girl probably returned from Iraq or Afghanistan, or maybe just missed deployment, and now she had to deal with this shit. He decided to not think about it, and focused on the task at hand.

"Take a right up ahead," he ordered. "That should take us downtown. At least I think it will...It's tough to match the location to the map with some of this damage."

"I think the hardware store's down this way, sir. Downtown was a couple blocks back."

"Fair enough. You'd know the area better than me. We'll circle back later, then."

"Yes, sir."

Collins put the night-vision scope back to his eyes. There were a few shops on the street, their windows and doors boarded over by the owners. Some had unnecessarily spray-painted the word "closed" across the wood and, in one case, part of the brick face of the store.

The ruins of the hardware store were at the end of the second block. The lumberyard was a scattered mess. A hand-written sign hung on the warped front door: "CLOSED UNTIL FURTHER NOTICE." Collins suppressed a laugh. He got a good look into the storage barn as they passed, and was surprised the owner would leave the doors open but hang a sign on the shop. There were stacks of materials inside; wide, flat stuff, maybe insulation boards or wall paneling. Most of the stacks were low, probably cleared out for reconstruction. There were a few rows of doors in the back, complete with frames, waiting for purchase.

Then he saw the corner of a canvas roof sticking out from the back. Collins bolted upright in the seat.

"Stop here," he ordered. "Right here!"

The private slammed on the brakes. The sudden stop jostled Collins, but it only took a second to find the roof again, and the tail end of a Jeep sticking out the back. He couldn't tell the color through the scope.

"Bingo. Pull in here."

"Found our target, sir?"

"There's a Jeep in that barn. It's either our guy or a looter."

Collins set down the night scope and moved his hand to the radio as the private backed up, turned the wheel, and moved into the parking lot. He aimed the headlights straight into the barn and hit the high beams, revealing the pale green edge of the Jeep.

"That's him!"

"What do we do, sir?" the Private asked.

"Hold that thought," Collins whispered. He lifted the radio to his mouth.

Beside him, the private suddenly slumped over the wheel.

"I wouldn't do that," a voice whispered in Collins' ear.

Collins dropped the radio and flung himself out the side of the Humvee. He hit the gravel shoulder first and rolled through the impact, gritting his teeth at the pain. Still crouched, he pulled the .45 from its holster and pointed it at the Humvee with both hands, searching for a target. Then he gasped.

The man in the white overcoat was crouched like a bird of prey in the back seat of the Humvee. His long coat was stretched over the seat like a cape. The vehicle still coasted forward, and he twisted at the same speed to face Collins. A lopsided grin played across his lips.

"Halt," Collins shouted. He thumbed the pistol's hammer back. "Right there, buddy. Get out of the vehicle!"

"Get out?" The man's grin grew wider, seeming to split his face. "But it's still moving. It's never wise to exit a moving vehicle."

Collins jumped to his feet.

"Don't worry about the girl." The man jerked his thumb over his shoulder. "She's just sleeping."

"I said get out of the vehicle! That's an order."

"Okay, okay! Don't get bitchy!" The man hopped out over the back. His long hair whipped about him. He flexed his knees as he landed, and slowly stood straight again. The Humvee rolled through the barn doors behind him. Private Gabriel, who was still slumped behind the wheel, never stirred.

"Who the hell are you?" Collins demanded. "What were you doing at the school?"

"Who am I? Well, if you insist on introductions, I've gone by many names. Some called me Malakh Ha-Mashhit, but that's just one of many. It depends on which language you speak, and what tome you're reading. Are you referring to the works of King James or Daniel? Or perhaps Frazer's *Golden Bough*? I appear in the uncondensed version under several different names. Or maybe you prefer the *Daemonolateria*? I've got more names than P. Diddy. Is P. Diddy still popular? It's hard to keep up with music these days. Maybe I should change that joke."

Collins opened his mouth to speak, and then shut it again. The guy was obviously crazy. If he said the wrong thing, it could make the man even more unstable.

"As for the school and what I'm doing here," the man continued, "I just wanted to see White Fire in action. Beautiful, isn't it?"

Collins felt the blood drain from his face. "How do you know that name?"

The man in the trench-coat laughed. "*Nobody* keeps secrets from me, Tommy."

This can't be right, Collins thought. *The guy has to be a spook, either ours or someone else's. Or Black Lodge, maybe? It's the only way he could know.*

And if he was someone else's operative, then maybe he was after a sample of the virus.

"Get down on the ground," Collins ordered, suddenly feeling cold.

The man frowned. "That's not gonna happen, Tommy."

Collins frowned. "How do you know my name?"

"The same way I knew White Fire's real name. Names are important, Tom."

"Not as important as the gun I have pointed at you. Get down on the ground and put your hands behind your fucking head. Now!"

"Hmm, let me think on that. Um...No."

The man stepped sideways as he spoke. His trench-coat billowed behind him. Collins tracked him with the pistol.

"God damn it, I *will* shoot you!"

"If you must. Do what you have to do, Tom."

Collins' finger tightened around the trigger. Palm sweat trickled through the grooves in the pistol grip. He could always shoot the man in the leg, then get the private's cuffs and haul him back to the school.

"Boo!" The man in the trench-coat leaped at Collins, his hands outstretched.

Collins gave a sharp cry and squeezed the trigger three times in rapid succession. His training came back like instinct and he absorbed the recoil in his wrist, putting three rounds into the man's center of mass. His ears rang in the aftermath, and his hands reverberated from the shock.

The assailant took a step back and looked down at the three smoking holes in his chest, one in his coat and two in his white shirt. No blood flowed from the wounds, though Collins could see he wasn't wearing a vest. The man poked a finger through the ragged hole in his lapel.

"This was an expensive coat, you asshole! Watch your aim next time."

Collins' eyes went wide, and his legs went weak. "What the...?"

"I'll take that." The man snatched the pistol out of Collins' grip. He released the magazine and let it fall to the ground, then kicked it and sent it flying across the parking lot. He fired the chambered bullet into the air and the slide locked back on the empty magazine slot. He then hurled the pistol over the fence into the next lot.

Collins gaped. "What...what are you?"

"Now *that* is the million-dollar question. And if you think hard on it, you might already know."

Collins shook his head slowly. His eyes darted left and right. He could flee, maybe make it past the man and out of the parking lot where he could make his way to the school, or he could turn and retreat into the barn and make for the Humvee and the M-16 between the seats. But he had seen this guy run. The man, or whatever he was, was too damned fast.

The lunatic laughed. "Oh, come on now. Think! You've been chasing me most of your life, Tom Collins. Ever since your dearest mother died of AIDS after that botched transfusion. 'Oh Mommy, boo hoo! I'm gonna grow up to be a big bad doctor so nobody dies of AIDS ever again!'"

"How can you know about that?" Collins backed away. His heel struck a piece of lumber on the ground. It was cracked down the center and useless for construction, but it would make a decent club. He imagined it would have no better effect than the bullets, but it was better than nothing. "Nobody knows about that."

"I do."

"How?"

"You're a country music fan, right, Tom? Johnny Cash sang about me on his last disc before he died. He got his lyrics from the Bible, of course. I believe the relevant chapter starts something like this. 'And I saw when the Lamb opened one of the seals, and I heard, as it were the noise of thunder, one of the four beasts saying, Come and see.' Ring any bells?"

Collins blinked. Could the man be an angel? No, surely not. But that would explain how the bullets had seemingly had no effect on him. And he knew so much. Knew Collins' name and knew about his mother—and about White Fire. And then there was that hallucination Collins had experienced upon first seeing him—the winds spreading out from behind his back.

"D-death?"

The man in the overcoat rolled his eyes. "No, I'm not Death. That old stick in the mud? He's not nearly as much fun as I am. Guess again."

"Pestilence?"

The man in the trench-coat winked and touched his fingertip to his nose. "Pleased to meet you. Hope you guessed my name. Johnny Cash should have covered that before he died."

"Bullshit."

"Bullshit that Johnny Cash should have covered The Rolling Stones?"

"You know what the hell I mean. You're not the Angel of Pestilence from the Bible."

"I'm hurt, Tom. Hurt that you don't believe me. Okay... maybe the Rolling Stones reference is a little dated, and sure, they wrote that about Lucifer, rather than me, but you could still show me a little respect. I'm the Ha-mashhit. I used to command the Mishlahat Malakhei Ra'im—the same band of angels who bore witness to the plagues of Egypt, back in the day. The Talmudic sages used to liken us to a wolf pack."

"Bullshit," Collins repeated.

"You saw me earlier tonight. Do you remember?"

"Yes," Collins admitted. "When we were driving. Revealed in the lightning, right before the tornado. It looked like..."

"What? Go on..."

"It looked like—for just a second—that you had wings... and a leering skull. But clearly, you don't."

"Are you sure?"

"You were there," Collins replied. "You were waiting for us on the side of the road when Phil and I passed through."

Pestilence yawned. "Nothing slips by you, does it, Tommy?"

"How did you know we were coming? Who told you our route?"

"Are you familiar with Irenaeus?"

"No." Collins shook his head.

"He was an influential second century Christian theologian. He called me the White Rider. So, let's just say that the White Rider wanted to see the White Fire for himself."

"This is your fault, isn't it," Collins demanded. "You caused the tornado, didn't you? You set the virus loose on these people!"

"Whoa, hey, let's not start pointing fingers." Pestilence held up his hands in mock surrender. "A second ago, you didn't even believe that I'm an angel. Now you're blaming me for everything, including the weather. Fact is, I'm just an observer. Nothing more. I didn't create this virus. And you know that. I didn't traipse it through a storm. That was all on you, Tom. You and McLeod. That was his name, right?"

"You don't get to say his name, fucker."

Pestilence waved the comment away. "You people always bring these things upon yourselves, and then you turn around and blame us for it. Ebola, AIDS, syphilis, cholera, hepatitis, even the frigging Plague. I bear witness to them all, but I didn't create them. He has given you brains so that you may think and hands so that you act. If you want to point a finger, you'd best turn it towards yourself."

Collins fumed. "Don't put this on me! I didn't know there would be a tornado."

"No, but you knew everything else, didn't you? April 18th, 2003, Captain. Does that date ring any bells? That was when you got the samples. You knew this virus was dangerous and deadly. The brass was even waiting on your recommendation. Destroy it? Store it? *Reproduce it?*"

"I said we should fight it, and save lives."

"That's right. Make a vaccine, you told them. Keep your boys in the fight! Be ready for anything, because *by God*, what if the *terrorists* got it? Smooth move, Tommy. How many lives are you saving now?"

"That's not how it happened. You're twisting everything around!"

"Am I? It sounds like a fair representation to me. And regardless of your motives, here we are. And all you had to do was retype one...small...paragraph. And boom! They would have wiped ol' White Fire off the face of the Earth."

"No. That's not true. We didn't know if it was secure. Anybody could have it, just like the Russian nukes that hit the arms markets! We were running scared. Ever since that terrorist group release the Purple Cloud over that town..."

"Yes." Pestilence nodded. I was there, too."

"If you were there, then you saw what happened. We couldn't take the same chance with White Fire. Like I said, we didn't know if it was secure."

"But you didn't bother to check, did you? Your government's crawling with intelligence services, but you didn't make one single phone call."

Collins sighed. "Okay. So, I fucked up. Is that what you want me to say? Is that what this is about? Fine, I fucked up. I dropped the ball. Now what? I go to Hell? You take my soul?"

Pestilence chuckled. "Got a little Catholic guilt going on, don't we?"

Collins glared. His fingers flexed. He touched his heel to the length of lumber to make sure he knew where it was. He had to move fast.

"Don't worry," Pestilence said. "That's not my call. And besides, God is Love, yes? You people have got the whole shiny, happy New Testament to help you sleep at night. Not that you believe in the New Testament, of course. And believe me, there are worse places to go than Hell. Try visiting the Void sometime. Ob and the Siqqusim make Satan and his minions look like a daycare center. Or try the Great Deep. Better take a life vest if you do, though."

Collins hovered over the length of wood.

"But you're not off the hook," the angel continued. "Not by a long shot, Captain. You might not be going to Hell, but I think it's only fair that you experience what you've put others through."

"You stay the fuck away from me, you crazy son of a bitch."

"Not a chance. You kept White Fire alive, and now you're going to feel the burn."

Pestilence stepped forward. Collins dropped to one knee and grabbed the end of the board, then lunged up and swung it around. The makeshift club caught the angel across the temple with a loud crack, and the board split in two. Collins dropped one section of splintered wood, and then swung the remaining segment in a vicious overhead arc. Pestilence blocked the blow with his forearm, but Collins hit him again, and again, and again.

The impacts reverberated through the club, stinging his hands. It was like beating solid steel. Jagged shards of wood dug into his palm and the undersides of his fingers, but he kept on swinging, altering from left to right to hit Pestilence on the shoulder, the elbow, and the side of his head. The angel took a step back, shrinking from the blows, and Collins took heart that he was winning.

"Okay," Pestilence growled. "This was fun, but that's about enough."

He caught the next blow in his palm and ripped the club out of Collins' hand. One splinter dug a long furrow through his lifeline and took a strip of flesh with it.

Screaming, Collins pressed his opposite thumb to the wound. Pestilence backhanded him, the blow like a sledgehammer to his jaw. He felt weightless for half a second before he landed on the gravel, then rolled face-first and slid on his chest. He slowly pushed himself up to his knees and grew worried when he couldn't feel the left side of his face.

Pestilence planted a foot in his ribs. It was just a nudge for the angel, but it sent him rolling, once, twice, three times and onto his back. The angel was on him before he could take a breath.

"Stop," Collins pleaded. "Please, stop."

"I don't think so, Tommy. Not a chance."

Buttons flew as Pestilence ripped the front of Collins' field jacket open. He tried to escape but his opponent pinned him to the ground with a knee to the hip. He took a swing at the angel's chin, and Pestilence rocked his head to one side and dodged the blow. A sharp punch in the gut knocked the wind out of Collins, and he didn't resist as the angel tore his uniform from his neck to his navel.

"Please," he managed. "Don't..."

"Hush," Pestilence soothed. "This will only take a minute."

The overcoat-wearing angel pressed his hand to Collins chest.

Collins screamed. His insides seemed to melt and surge upward. It felt like a sword, pushing through his body from the inside, and he felt a warm wetness trickle around his ribs. He screamed and cried, hoping somebody would come to his aid, but there was nothing. He didn't want to die, and he writhed and kicked, but the angel held him fast. The pain spiked higher and higher as his heart pressed against his sternum, and then he *did* want to die, anything to make the pain end.

And then it stopped.

His muscles went slack and hit the ground, woozy but without the energy to throw up. He felt his heart slide back into place and start beating again. His lungs pulled in great gasps of air and he struggled to keep from hyperventilating.

"There." Pestilence wiped his palms on Collins' pants and stood. "That should do it."

"What have you done to me?" The words escaped Collins' lips as little more than a papery whisper.

"Your antibodies against the virus are gone. You're going to get very sick, Tommy. And very soon."

"W-white Fire?"

Pestilence nodded, then turned and walked toward the barn.

"Oh God," Collins moaned. "Oh my God…"

"He's not listening," Pestilence called over his shoulder. "He never listens anymore. His answering machine is turned off."

"Wait!" Collins shouted. He struggled up to one elbow and coughed. "Are these the…the end times?"

The angel laughed, loud and hard. Then he stopped and turned. "You mean as in the Book of Revelations? A lot of that symbolism is just plain wrong, my friend. You people believe it to be the inspired word of God, but meanwhile, it's just the ramblings of a madman. A lunatic! The apostle John was pretty fucked up when he wrote that screed, and by fucked up, I don't mean on hallucinogens, either. No way. See, he'd just spent five of your Earth years wandering the Labyrinth."

"I don't understand what you're saying."

"And you don't need to. What you need to know is that John got it wrong, and you people have continued getting it wrong ever since then. The apocalypse that John wrote of doesn't happen in the blink of an eye. The seals don't go all at once. They are events, some from before A.D. 95, when John wrote it, and the others after that time. He was seeing into the future, trying to predict it. But none of you understand the timetable."

"But why does it have to happen at all?"

Pestilence paused before responding. "My brothers and I have been here a long, long time. We are tired of waiting. So, we're bringing about the end ourselves. If we don't do it, then the Thirteen will. They've already laid waste to several other realities. Soon they will focus on this one. The end could come via darkness or the dead rising or a global deluge, but none of those things would serve God. Our way does."

"I still don't understand," Collins said.

"Nor will you. There are many things which you are not privy to. Here is just one of them. You ready for this? God is not whole. He is not sitting on His throne in Heaven—at least, not entirely. We are acting in His stead until He returns. We've been doing so for quite some time. Ever since the events at Calvary. And while we're hard at work on this, the Thirteen are hard at work their way, and Satan and his minions in Hell are at it, as well. Three different groups, all trying to bring about the end of humanity."

"W-why?"

Pestilence shrugged. "It depends on the group. The forces of Hell are doing it because they want to enslave and rule over you. The Thirteen are doing it because they're nihilistic assholes. As for my kind? We believe this is the only way. This is what our Creator would have wanted. This was all put into place a long time ago. As I said, humanity doesn't understand the timetable. Some of the seals have already happened. As for the fifth seal...well, let's just say we're getting there."

A second dizzy spell overcame Collins and he lay back down. His lips felt numb, and his ears rang. He heard an engine start, and wheels rumbling through the gravel behind him. Then it was gone.

He passed out shortly thereafter.

14

"Sir? Captain Collins? Wake up, sir!"

Collins winced as someone gently slapped his face. He opened one eye and glimpsed Private Gabriel hovering above him. Her expression was one of concern.

"Sir? Can you hear me?"

Groaning, Collins sat up abruptly and shoved the young woman away from him.

"Sorry, Captain," Gabriel apologized. "I thought you were dead!"

"I thought I was, too."

"You're hurt. Do you want me to call for a medic? The radio in the Humvee still works."

Ignoring the question, Collins glanced around in confusion. They were still in the ruined hardware store's parking lot, and it was still nightfall.

"What happened?"

"I don't know, sir. I think we had an accident. The Humvee is wrecked, but drivable. I must have been knocked unconscious. I woke up behind the wheel. Then I found you laying here."

"How long were we out?"

"A half hour, tops." Gabriel pointed to the ground. "You discharged your weapon, sir. Did you engage our target?"

Collins followed her gaze. Sure enough, empty brass casings littered the cracked pavement. Collins glanced up at the sky, and shrugged.

"I—I don't remember anything, sir. What happened to us?"

Collins didn't answer. He rolled onto his side and then slowly got to his feet.

"Captain, I'm not sure you should be moving! Your chest..."

Collins looked down and saw dried blood in the shape of a handprint on his chest. The thumb hooked just under his right nipple and the fingers fanned out across his pecs. The palm neatly obscured most of his sternum. Dried blood trails encircled his ribs, and a dark, purple bruise ran between the fingers and surrounded the hand.

"I'll be okay," he replied. "You said the Humvee is operational?

"I believe so, sir."

"Go get it then. On the double."

"Yes, sir!" The private ran into the barn and returned with the vehicle a moment later.

"Take me back to the school." Collins climbed into the passenger seat and sagged into it. His chest felt like he'd been lying under a boulder, and he could hardly keep his eyes open as he rested against the headrest. Every bump in the road sent pain shooting through his shoulders, neck, and skull.

When they drove back over the bloody cow carcass, he passed out.

***

When Collins entered the school lobby, assisted by Private Gabriel, the first person he saw was Colonel Sharpe, rushing toward him.

"I was advised you were coming in," the commanding officer said. "Jesus Christ, Tom! What the hell happened to you?" Collins took a deep breath, which caused a horrible stabbing pain in his side. How should he answer? He couldn't very well tell the Colonel that he'd run into one of the Four Horsemen of the Apocalypse.

"We had an accident," he lied. "Spotted the guy and his Jeep, but then we seemed to have...hit something. Wreckage or debris from the storm."

A paramedic and a military doctor pushed a stretcher to his side and gently helped Collins lie down, with some assistance from Private Gabriel. The doctor immediately started poking at his chest and pressed a cold stethoscope to his ribs.

"And your target," Sharpe demanded. "What of him?"

"He escaped, sir," Private Gabriel answered before Collins could reply. "Permission to renew efforts to find him?"

"Standby, Private...?"

She snapped off a salute. "Gabriel, sir."

"Are you injured, as well?"

"No, sir. I don't seem to be."

"Well, all the same, I want you to get checked out. If the doctors approve it, then find your commanding officer and tell them to form up a team with you. Tell them that's an order straight from me. I admire your determination, but you can't go out there alone."

"Copy that, sir."

Collins reached out and took Gabriel's hand. She stared down at him, surprised.

"Did they vaccinate you and the rest of your unit before deploying you to Godfrey?"

She nodded. "yes, sir."

Collins smiled. "Good. When you get home, you give your husband and your kid a hug, okay?"

Gabriel returned the smile. "That's affirmative, Captain.'

Collins watched as the medical team led her away. Then he looked back up at Sharpe.

"This is a clusterfuck, Tom. Tell me you've got something—anything—for me."

Collins frowned, thinking. "I've got his name."

"You do?"

Collins nodded weakly. "It's Malakh Ha-Mashhit. But it might be an alias. And he uses other aliases, as well."

Sharpe pulled a small tablet and a pen from his pocket and jotted the information down. "I'll get this to Homeland. See what they can dig up."

Collins nodded again, bemused at the idea of the Department of Homeland Security finding anything on Pestilence.

"Get some rest," Sharpe told him. "I want a full sit rep after they've patched you up."

"Copy that, sir."

The doctors pushed Collin down the hall, still poking and prodding him. He assured them the pain was an ache, not a sharp pain, and nothing was broken, but they were intent on seeing for themselves. They scrubbed the blood off his chest—a painful process in itself—and, ultimately, agreed that yes, he had a contusion but no real damage. Meanwhile the paramedic extracted the splinters from his hand, cleaned the wounds with alcohol, and bound his palm with gauze.

When they finally left him, Collins sagged into the cot and closed his eyes.

"So," a gruff voice asked, "what's White Fire?"

Collins lifted his head and saw Chief Hansen lying on another cot near the wall. The big man had propped himself up on one elbow to face Collins, and he had an IV connected to his right arm.

Collins licked his lips, trying to speak. "Is that..."

"Yep." Hansen held up his arm and turned the intravenous tube slowly, as if showing off a new tattoo. "The fever and headache started about an hour ago. No sense taking chances, I figure."

"Are you okay?"

"You tell me, Captain."

Collins changed the subject. "How'd you hear the name? White Fire?"

"Sharpe. I overheard it a couple times, but when I asked him about it, he did his best Helen Keller impression."

"Oh."

"You owe me, Collins." Hansen swung his legs over the side of the cot and sat up, wincing as he did. "And don't try to pull that classified shit on me, either. I think I earned a right to know!"

Collins lay back down and covered his eyes with his forearm to block out the light. At this point, he just didn't give a shit anymore. The press would file a Freedom of Information request for every scrap of paper in the Pentagon, followed quickly by a federal investigation and maybe even a Congressional inquiry. He fully expected to have a microscope embedded in his ass for the next day or two.

Assuming he lived that long.

"It's Russian," he replied at last. "They called it White Fire. We simply called it Viral Meningitis Mark II, or VM2 for short. Not as romantic-sounding name, but this virus wasn't very romantic anyway. It's a weaponized strain of an enterovirus, designed to spread through the air and work fast. Highly transmissible, and there's no cure."

Hansen groaned. "None at all?"

"Like I told you back when we first met, there's a vaccine, to protect humans from contracting the virus. But if it gets in your system before you've taken the vaccine, it's unstoppable. Spreads like wildfire."

"Fuck me…"

"Yeah," Collins agreed.

"How…how many people have been vaccinated?"

Collins shrugged. "All of our troops in Afghanistan, Iraq, South Korea, Iran and the other hotspots. A few hundred more here in the States. And probably all of those on duty here tonight."

Chief Hansen coughed. "Why so few?"

"Simple. It's a numbers game. We just don't have enough

vaccine yet."

"No stockpiles?" Hansen broke into another fit of coughing.

"There were budget cuts," Collins explained.

"Jesus Christ. So, it's just going to keep on going?"

"Not necessarily. The Soviets first used it near the end of their war with Afghanistan. Unfortunately, it worked a little too well, and wiped out a village before their mujahedeen fathers and husbands returned. They bottled it up and set it aside for further research, but then the Iron Curtain fell. Fast forward to 2003. We get wind of it, and the concern then was who else has the virus? If one of the terror networks got a sample, either from the Russian arms market or the village, it could be disastrous. But...then we changed presidents, and there were budget cuts, and White Fire got shelved in storage. Until earlier this year."

"What changed?"

"You remember when terrorists released that purple gas in that small town?"

The Chief nodded.

"That was a wake-up call, even more so than September eleventh. Before that, we were worried about civilian aircraft and suicide bombers and truck attacks. After that, we began focusing earnestly on chemical and biological threats. McLeod and I were on the way to a CDC facility near Morris, Illinois to start research on a White Fire vaccine for the general population, in case there's an attack. The budget finally got approved. Everything was a go."

Hansen chuckled, but there was no humor in it. "And before you could do it, the tornado set it loose. Wonderful."

"This is the United States, not some third-world dirt village. The damage will be contained."

"Yeah? Tell that to the people we've carted out of here in body bags so far. Tell that to their *families*, who may never even be able to give their loved ones a proper burial! Tell it to Chris Brannon. He was just a kid! Tell it to…"

The Chief broke off into a round of coughing. Collins waited patiently for it to subside. The Chief glared at him, wheezing.

"You're gonna burn for this, Collins. Trust me on that. The media's going to have you all twisting in the wind."

"Tell me something I don't know." Collins rolled to his side and turned his back on the big man. "Good night, Chief."

Chief Hansen answered with another cough.

***

Collins woke slowly. An intense headache squeezed the back of his skull, pounding his head and neck with every heartbeat. The soft morning light streaming through the windows felt like it was cooking him where he lay. The grogginess dispelled like a fog and he shouted for help.

A pair of doctors burst into the room and ran to his side.

"White Fire," he told them. "I've got it!"

"That's impossible. You've been vaccinated." The doctor pressed a thermometer into his ear. It trilled a second later and the doctor examined the readout. "Holy shit..."

Doctors swarmed him, taking blood samples and administering injections and shoving an IV into his arm. Someone taped a bag of ice to his chest and he swore he could feel it boiling to steam. The doctors all barked orders and shouted vital stats, but it all reduced to fuzzy, white noise. He saw red through his eyelids, then black.

There were less of them when he came to again. A soldier in a bio-suit rolled him onto his side, then shoved his knees to his chest. He didn't resist. Most meningitis patients only endured a spinal tap for diagnostic purposes, but the Army doctors learned quick that White Fire moved fast enough it was best to relieve the cranial pressure by draining fluid.

The antibiotic cleanser felt cool on his back. The puncture

would hurt like hell, but he didn't care if it would let the molten lead out of his skull.

The doctor in front of him gripped his hand. "Are you okay to do this?"

Collins had been about to shake his head emphatically yes, but then realized the doctor was talking to the man behind him. The man with the needle.

"It has to be done." The voice was familiar.

"Your hands are trembling."

That wasn't what Collins wanted to hear. He struggled to look over his shoulder.

"I'm going in," the man with the needle said, and Collins caught a glimpse of his long, white hair.

"Wait," the doctor shouted. "You're too high!"

"Relax, Tommy," Pestilence whispered. "You won't feel a thing down there. I promise."

Searing white pain lanced Collins' back. His screams rattled the windows.

15

Two Years Later

Collins flashed his identification at the checkpoint. The shack guard examined it, then smiled and waved him on through. He drove on up the service road to the main building, utilizing the controls on the steering column. His legs were useless, and the vehicle accommodated his disability. He parked in his designated space, and set to work getting the wheelchair out of the back seat. Once he was settled in, he rolled to the trunk. He glanced around before opening it, then pulled out a pair of oblong gray oxygen bottles and strapped them to the mounts on the side of his chair.

He was the only person involved in the Godfrey incident to have contracted White Fire and lived. His colleagues said that was because he'd been vaccinated, but Collins wasn't so sure.

There was a palm print on his chest, faded, like old scar tissue, but always there. A tattooed reminder of what he'd helped unleash. The handprint itched at night, and sometimes Collins still got phantom headaches.

He didn't much care for civilian life. Between the media, the investigations, and the rehabilitation and physical therapy, the first year had been tough on him. The Army discharged him on disability. He appealed, but it became clear he was lucky to land an honorable discharge and keep his clearance status. But he wanted to be back in the labs.

He *needed* to be.

It took some time, but he finally landed a job working for DefenseMed, a division of the Globe Corporation that was doing research work for the Department of Defense. His background, education and security clearances landed him a fat salary and he wondered if he should have left the military sooner. DefenseMed also had a lot more toys for him to play with, and a little more freedom to experiment.

The light foot traffic in the hallways cleared the way as he negotiated his way to the Infectious Diseases department. An armed guard greeted him at the door and inspected his identification.

"Good morning, Dr. Collins. Running late today?"

"A little bit. How's it going, George?"

"No complaints. What you got there?" The guard nodded toward the bottle strapped to the side of the wheelchair.

"O2."

"What, DefenseMed's oxygen not good enough for you?"

Collins let out an obligatory chuckle. "No, it's not like that. The tanks and the suit hookups are bulky. Hard to do it in this wheelchair. Thought I'd give this a try and see how it works."

The guard leaned over and rapped a knuckle against the side. It rang through the interior of the tank. He harrumphed, and then turned on his scanning wand. It beeped in all the usual places around the chair. The guard gently lifted each of Collins' useless legs in turn, scanned them, and carefully replaced them.

"You're all set, Doc. Have a nice day."

"You too, George. Later."

Collins rolled onward, into the Infectious wing. He greeted a few coworkers, and then struggled into the white clean suit and respirators all the techs wore. One of the other doctors chatted with him about the results of a few tests with a staphylococcus strain, then thankfully left him alone.

If George the guard had been a little more thorough, he might have noticed the two bottles were joined together at the tops. Collins cranked them open, pressurizing the second bottle with the first. The second had another small valve in the bottom, which in turn connected to the pipe concealed within the framework of his wheelchair.

Collins rolled his wheels manually and did not touch the electronic controls mounted near his left hand. He had replaced it just last night with a duplicate box that performed a different function altogether.

The cryogenic lab was just ahead. Collins rolled straight up the small handicap access ramp DefenseMed had been gracious enough to build for him, then went right through the airlock and into the lab without bothering to don the protective gear.

A doctor in a bio-suit—he couldn't tell who through the mask—turned and let out a shocked gasp when he saw Collins sitting there unprotected. "Are you crazy? You can't be in here like that!"

"Get the fuck out of here," Collins growled.

"We have to quarantine you, right away!" The doctor lunged for an alarm button.

"Suit yourself." Collins leaned down and flipped open the valve at the bottom of the second tank, then aimed the wheelchair at the equipment lining the walls.

"Never again, you little bastards," he whispered. "You're gonna burn."

Collins slapped a pair of switches on the mock control unit. It had been a lot easier than he thought to replace the oxygen with fuel, and the valves worked flawlessly. The pressurized air in the first tank pushed the fuel in the second tank through the concealed tubes to the electric igniter. The igniter created a small arc within the nozzle mounted to the tip of the chair's armrest, lighting the stream of fuel an instant before it sprayed into the room.

Sheets of flame washed across the walls, shelves, and refrigerated cabinets. Alarms went off and the sprinklers heads burst. The other doctor shouted for help and disappeared into the airlock.

Collins painted the room with more flames. The oily fuel clung to everything, and the water didn't have a prayer of putting it out any time soon. Security guards pounded on the windows behind him, threatening to shoot.

He ignored it all, and laughed as the viruses burned in white-hot fire.

ABOUT THE AUTHOR

BRIAN KEENE writes novels, comic books, short fiction, and occasional journalism for money. He is the author of over forty books, mostly in the horror, crime, and dark fantasy genres.

Keene also hosts the popular podcast The Horror Show with Brian Keene, which airs weekly on iTunes, iHeartRadio, Spotify, Stitcher, and elsewhere via the Project Entertainment Network.

Keene's 2003 novel, *The Rising*, is often credited (along with Robert Kirkman's *The Walking Dead* comic and Danny Boyle's *28 Days Later* film) with inspiring pop culture's current interest in zombies.

In addition to his own original work, Keene has written for media properties such as *Doctor Who*, *The X-Files*, *Hellboy*, *Masters of the Universe*, and *Alien*.

Several of Keene's novels have been developed for film, including *Ghoul*, *The Naughty List*, *The Ties That Bind*, and *Fast Zombies Suck*. Several more are in-development or under option. Keene also served as Executive Producer for *I'm Dreaming of a White Doomsday*.

Keene also oversees Maelstrom, his own small press publishing imprint specializing in collectible limited editions, via Thunderstorm Books.

Keene's work has been praised in such diverse places as *The New York Times*, *The History Channel*, *The Howard Stern Show*, *CNN.com*, *Publisher's Weekly*, *Media Bistro*, *Fangoria Magazine*, and *Rue Morgue Magazine*.

He has won numerous awards and honors, including the 2017 Necon Legend Award, the 2016 Imadjinn Award for Best Fantasy Novel, the 2015 Imaginarium Film Festival Awards for Best Screenplay, Best Short Film Genre, and Best

Short Film Overall, the 2014 World Horror Grandmaster Award, 2001 Bram Stoker Award for Nonfiction, 2003 Bram Stoker Award for First Novel, 2004 Shocker Award for Book of the Year, and Honors from United States Army International Security Assistance Force in Afghanistan and Whiteman A.F.B. (home of the B-2 Stealth Bomber) 509th Logistics Fuels Flight.

A prolific public speaker, Keene has delivered talks at conventions, college campuses, theaters, and inside Central Intelligence Agency headquarters in Langley, VA.

Keene serves on the Board of Directors for the Scares That Care 501c charity organization.

The father of two sons, Keene lives in rural Pennsylvania.

CPSIA information can be obtained
at www.ICGtesting.com
Printed in the USA
BVHW041341140719
553412BV00010B/53/P

9 781621 052777